PREVIEW

"**D**id you see the outfit Ashley was wearing today? It looked like she needed a shoehorn to get it on." Seventeen-year-old Lauren said and started to laugh.

Everyone at the table started laughing, too.

"I know, I don't know why she doesn't go on a diet. Why would she let herself get that fat?" I mean, just stop eating already, right?" Miranda said, shrugging her shoulders.

Jaycee rubbed her hands together. "She'd have more friends if she didn't look like such a pig, right? Like, who wants to be seen with her when they go out places? It's like embarrassing and all. I know I would be anyway, I don't know about you guys."

Rebecca had had enough. "Guys, listen to me, she has a medical problem and has to take medication. The medication saves her life, but it causes her to gain weight. She eats no more food than you or I and she tries to exercise more than we do. She can't help it. We should be her friend and give her support and encouragement, not be her enemies and talk mean and cruel behind her back.

Jaycee cocked her head to one side. "She really can't help it and doesn't eat a lot?"

"NO, she doesn't. She really can't help it."

"Oh man, that's tough. I feel bad I came down so rough and judgmental on her." Jaycee said, furrowing her eyebrows.

Lauren looked down at the table. "I guess my comment was really mean. I shouldn't have said it."

Miranda looked around the table and then stared down at her hands. "I guess I should be more embarrassed at my comment than being embarrassed by being seen with her. I'm awful, I guess."

Jaycee looked across the room. "Hey look, she just came into the lunchroom and is sitting over there. Why don't we invite her to sit with us?"

Rebecca smiled and stood up. "I will go and get her."

She walked over to where Ashley was sitting alone. "Hey, everyone wants you to come and sit with us over there."

Ashley's eyes opened wide. "REALLY, for real? They want me to eat with them?" Well, O. K!"

They walked over to the table and sat down. They looked at what Ashley was eating. She was eating a salad with grilled chicken, an apple, carrots, and a bottle of vegetable juice. They looked sheepishly at their own trays. Everyone else was eating pizza, fruit punch, potato chips, and cookies.

"Hi Ashley, how are you? I'm glad you can eat with us. Maybe you can hang out with us after school today because we are all going over to Jaycee's house to go swimming." Lauren said.

Ashley's eyes grew big. "That would be great because swimming is great exercise, thank you very much for inviting me!"

"Yeah, we do a lot of things together and you can join us, it will be fun," Miranda said.

Ashley nodded her head. "That would be so much fun and I would love it and would love to have you guys as friends!"

Rebecca was glad her friends could see the truth behind Ashley's weight and listen to her explanation. It was wonderful they were going to include her in their friendship group. Ashley would no longer be an outsider, alone in the world and she was no longer bullied in school.

The Things

I Never Knew

A Novella

By

Jennifer Ann Corgan

DEDICATION

I dedicate this book to EVERY man, woman, boy and girl out there who does not know their true worth, who looks down on themselves with scorn. You are beautiful, you are amazing and you are real. Don't look to the world for your value, look to your heavenly Father who loves you so very much. His Son died for you so you can be free. Rejoice, and be who you are and be the person who changes the world in small, yet important ways. You will never know the impact you had on the world until you are with your heavenly father but know that helping others and encouraging others will make Him smile. Give more than you take and give with your whole heart and reach out to others less fortunate than you or who don't know their value in God's eyes. You may turn a doubting and shy person into someone who changes the world. Let your light shine and let the world know that you are there to set it on fire and to change it in extraordinary ways.

God is good and wants good things for you. He wants you to then share that goodness with others. You may just change the world.

TABLE OF CONTENTS

DEDICATION 7

CHAPTER ONE 11

CHAPTER TWO 15

CHAPTER THREE 25

CHAPTER FOUR.. 34

CHAPTER FIVE 49

CHAPTER SIX.. 68

CHAPTER SEVEN 86

CHAPTER EIGHT 93

CHAPTER NINE... 108

CHAPTER TEN... 122

CHAPTER ELEVEN 131

CHAPTER TWELVE 142

CHAPTER THIRTEEN 151

COMING SOON SHATTERED FAMILY 154

MORE BOOKS BY JENNIFER ANN CORGAN 156

CHAPTER ONE

The roads were icy and slick as Rebecca's car drove down them at fifty miles an hour. She knew she should be going slower, but she wanted to get home for her TV show at 8:00 and she was cutting it close at 7:52. She still had a few more miles to go. She drove around a curve and turned her steering wheel but her tires continued going forward. She jerked the steering wheel, but the car didn't respond and she kept going forward toward a guard rail that overlooked a high incline that went down to large rocks and boulders at the bottom. The car hit the guardrail going fifty miles an hour and flipped over and tumbled down the incline. Rebeca screamed and clutched the steering wheel as her head was slammed back and forth against the window while the car rolled down the incline and banged against the rocks. It came to the bottom with a crash and Rebecca's head smashed against the steering wheel with such force that it split wide open. She died immediately.

****

Rebecca opened her eyes and saw a bright light. It was the brightest light she had ever seen and was the most beautiful, warm, loving, and inviting light. She was compelled to go towards it. She remembered the accident and wondered what had happened and where she was. She looked behind her and down below her was the accident scene, her car was all smashed up and her body was lying in the driver's seat with her head busted up and covered with blood. She realized she was dead and looked down at her current body. It was glowing and had a white pearly essence to it. She looked back at her mangled body and realized she died because she wanted to watch a TV show, a feeling of horror came over her and she knelt down and started to cry. Then she heard a voice.

"Rebecca, Come."

Rebecca looked up. The voice was coming from the bright light. The light was full of love and was inviting her. She stood up and walked toward it and she had to shield her eyes from the radiant light. She looked back again but only for a second and then proceeded forward into the light. It enveloped her and wrapped itself around her completely. She had never experienced such love and warmth and peace. Then she heard the voice again.

"Rebecca, You are home."

Rebecca looked up and saw the most beautiful face she had ever seen. It was so beautiful and loving and she had to glance away because she felt so unworthy to gaze at him. She got down on her knees before the face and put her face to the ground. Then she felt a hand on her head, lifting her face up. She looked into the face of love and tears came to her eyes. He looked at her with such tenderness and care, with such mercy and peace. He took her hand and had her stand up. He put a white robe around her shoulders.

"You are a princess," He said. "Well done my good and faithful servant. You are home." And He put a crown on her head.

But Rebecca thought she was unworthy. She touched the crown on her head and she rubbed the soft and luxurious robe on her shoulders. She did not feel like a good and faithful servant. She did not think she did anything that could be called well done. *I was not a good Christian when I was alive. I did not go to church faithfully on Sundays. I did not always put money into the offering. I did not really help those in need. I didn't adopt a Compassion orphan. I did not support missions in Church. I did not visit those in prison. I did not set a captive free. I did not lead anyone to Christ. In fact, she thought, I didn't help one person in my entire life. I did not make one difference in the world. I did not change the world at all for the better. I was a good person, and I existed in the world, but that was it, she thought.* She hung her head down low in shame.

The beautiful melodious voice and glorious face reached out His hand and raised her head up to gaze at Him. "Rebecca, you have done more than you know. You wouldn't be here otherwise."

Rebecca shook her head. "I have done nothing good. I took more than I gave. I was angry and belligerent and I was spiteful and mean. I was unforgiving and unloving and I didn't give people grace but I expected it for myself. I expected people to do for me and help me but I was never there for others. I was selfish and self-centered and stingy. Oh, Jesus, I was anything but good."

He put His glorious glowing hand on her head and His gentle and kind eyes had tears of compassion in them for her. He stared at her for a moment. "Rebecca, Rebecca, I am going to show you all you have done and what you have contributed to the world and what the world is like with you in it. I am also going to show you a world without you in it and what it would have been like without your impact. I will show you both so you can see what you have done in this world and for this world. We will take a journey together, just you and I."

Rebecca stood up next to Him, and He held out His arms as she rushed into them. He held her in His arms for what seemed like an eternity. All her fears and pain left her, and she looked forward to the journey he promised her. She wanted her disbelief to vanish, and she wanted to believe His words about her. Soon, he broke their embrace and took her arm in His and they walked down a golden road sprinkled with diamonds and precious gems, there were huge gold-gilded mansions on either side of them and beautiful beings walking about. They walked down a tunnel and sat on a huge cliff overlooking the world. They looked over the world and a scene opened before them.

CHAPTER TWO

"You are a fat, ugly pig, Ashley and you are ugly as a cow," Steven said as he threw some dirt at the ten-year-old little girl.

Ashley brushed the dirt off her face and walked along the street to the bus stop. Steven followed behind her, pretending to walk like an elephant, taking big, wide steps. Every so often, he stepped on the back of her sneakers, making her foot come out. She had to stop to push her foot back into the sneaker.

"Stop it, Steven. Please leave me alone. I've done nothing to you. You're so mean to me."

Steven smirked. "It's because you're such an ugly loser."

Ashley's eyes filled with tears that threatened to run down her cheeks.

Ashley was short for her age, four foot four, and weighed 130 pounds which was a lot for a seven-year-old. She had long brown, curly hair that hung to the middle of her back. Her deep brown eyes were large with long thick eyelashes. Her button nose was cute and so were her rosebud pink lips contrasting her creamy white skin. She was an attractive child except for her excessive weight which distorted her pretty features. Her stomach stuck out and she had rolls of fat on her back. Though she was seven, the weight caused her to have breasts that stuck out and she tried to wear loose-fitting shirts to hide them. Her legs were thick and her arms were wide and she had a double chin below cheeks that were rosy, round, and full. They caused her eyes to look squished on her face. She was a prime target for abuse and bullying.

They got to the bus stop and there were four other kids there. Steven continued to torment Ashley and Paul, Braydon, and Jason joined him.

"Ashley, Ashley, ugly, Ashley, fat and disgusting Ashley," said Paul as he stuck out his tongue at her and reached out and pinched her on the arm.

"Ouch. That hurt. Stop it. Please. Stop being so mean to me. Please." Ashley begged them.

Jason walked up to her and grabbed her backpack off her back and threw it up in the air and Braydon caught it.

"Give it back to me. Please give me back my backpack." She jumped up and tried to catch her bag but they kept throwing it above her head. They kept doing this until Braydon swung it and hit her across the face with it.

"Owwww. That hurt a lot. Ouch. You hit my face hard." She put her backpack back on her back and backed away from him.

Paul moved forward and tried to pull it back off of her and knocked her to the ground. She scraped her knee and it started to bleed, then she got hysterical.

"I'm bleeding! You made me bleed, why did you make me bleed? You're a bad, bad person!"

Just then, ten-year-old Rebecca walked down the road and joined the group. She saw Ashley down on the ground, crying with a bleeding knee. She rushed over to her.

"What happened Ashley? How did you fall down and get hurt?"

"The boys were being mean to me and pushed me down and were keeping my backpack from me. I'm bleeding now and I'm scared!"

Rebecca helped her stand up and turned and faced the boys.   "Don't touch her again or be mean to her again or you will have to deal with me. Got it?"

Paul smirked. "Yeah, you and what army? What are you going to do about it, Rebecca? I'm bigger than you and can beat you up." He came up to her and pushed her to the ground.

Rebecca got up and brushed off her shorts. She walked up to Paul and pushed him back hard and grabbed his backpack and swung it around and pushed. Paul lost his footing and fell to the ground hard. Everyone laughed when he fell. He got up quickly with a red face and grabbed his backpack and stood and faced Rebecca. He was at least a foot taller than her. He swung his hand and smacked her in the face. She rubbed the red spot on her face but did not back down. Paul stared at her for a moment and raised his eyebrows. Everyone looked at Rebecca with astonishment. Just then, the bus came and everyone got on. Rebecca sat with Ashley.

Later that day on the playground, Braydon and Jason were bullying Ashley again.

"Look at the fat little pig trying to play skip rope. Look at the earth shake. EARTHQUAKE!" Jason said quite loudly.

Ashley stopped jumping and her face turned bright red.

Braydon grabbed the jump rope from her and whipped it around so it hit her legs. "Ouch! That hurt. Stop hitting me. That's mean and you are big meanies."

"Ooooh, we are big meanies, " he said. "The big fat pig said we are big meanies." He swung the rope and hit Ashley again on her bare legs.

She screamed loudly this time. Braydon looked around to see if anyone was looking and when he saw no one, he did it again. She yelled again, a little softer this time.

"Why don't you lose some weight? Why are you so fat when you are only seven years old? You'll be a thousand pounds by the time you are a teenager." Then he roared with laughter and so did Jason. They had drawn a small crowd, and those who were watching also laughed. Ashley's face was bright red, and she had tears running down her face. She was extremely overweight, and she knew it. She had a serious medical condition and took medication to save her life, and the medication was what caused her to gain weight. She ate very little food, and she tried to get exercise as much as she could and that was why she was jumping rope today. But she could not help being the size that she was.

"I can't help being big. My medicine makes me fat."

"Oooooh, so your medicine makes you a fat pig. Not that you stuff your face with food. Yeah, right, Ashley. I doubt anyone believes that. You are a fat disgusting pig."

Ashley wanted to run away from them but she had to get her jump rope back because her mother would get very mad if she lost it.

"Give me back my jump rope, please."

"Come and get it." And he held it up high and laughed.

She walked up to him and jumped but could not reach the rope. He spun around, making her jump around in circles. Then he heard a voice.

"Give it back to her now."

He turned around, and it was Rebecca.

"Why should I?"

"Because I said so" And she walked right up to him and faced him several inches from his body.

He took a few steps back, and she took a few steps forward. She reached out and pinched his nipple on his chest.

"Owwwww, why the heck did you do that?"

"I said to give her back her jump rope, and I meant it."

Then she kneed him hard in the groin and he doubled over. "I can't believe you just did that to me, you little brat, here's the stupid jump rope."

"No, YOU are going to hand the jump rope to Ashley. Come here, Ashley."

Ashley came up to him and he handed the jump rope to her.

"And you aren't going to pick on her again, are you?"

He didn't answer, so she grabbed his nipple again, and he howled. "Are you?"

"No, I won't pick on her again."

"You promise her?." She reached to grab it again.

"Yes, I promise her."

Ashley turned to her. "Thank you for sticking up for me and for being my friend, Rebecca."

Rebecca smiled. "You're welcome. You're a nice girl. My mommy tells me it's what's on the inside that counts and it doesn't matter what we look like on the outside and I think you look just fine, Ashley. You are beautiful just as you are. I will be your friend for always."

They smiled at each other and held hands as they left the playground and walked into the school.

****

The next day Paul was on the bus and he was sitting behind Ashley and was pulling her hair.

"Ouch, stop pulling my hair." She sat forward so he couldn't get her.

Then he started sending spitballs over to her and they landed in her hair and on her clothes. She picked them off as they flew over. Jason and Michael joined in on the torture of Ashley and soon it was a constant barrage of spitballs coming over the seat onto her hair, and clothes.

Ashley was crying as she pulled the pieces of wet, spit-covered paper off of her clothes and hair. Rebecca was sitting two rows up and happened to glance back when she heard laughing. She saw what they were doing to Ashley. She stood up from her seat, came forward, and sat down next to her. Just then a big wad of spit-soaked paper landed on her cheek. Livid, she stood up and faced the boys. The boy's eyes were wide open, not expecting her to stand up to them..

"Cut it out now and believe me, I mean it."

Michael and Jason laughed and lobbed another volley of spitballs at them. Rebecca nodded her head and looked into her backpack. She brought out a box of apple juice and opened it up. She stood up, faced them, pointed the straw at them, and squeezed the box as hard as she could. Juice splattered the boys all over their faces, arms, backpacks, and clothes. They yelled and cursed as she moved her hand back and forth, ensuring all of them got wet and when it was empty, she stood there watching them.

"Are you done with your spitballs now?"

They looked at her with wide, angry, but astonished eyes. They certainly had a fierce opponent in Rebecca. They sat back in their seats, wiping the apple juice from their faces and clothes, and left Ashley alone for the rest of the bus ride.

****

"Did you see the outfit Ashley was wearing today? It looked like she needed a shoehorn to get it on." Seventeen-year-old Lauren said and started to laugh.

Everyone at the table started laughing, too.

"I know, I don't know why she doesn't go on a diet. Why would she let herself get that fat?" I mean, just stop eating already, right?" Miranda said, shrugging her shoulders.

Jaycee rubbed her hands together. "She'd have more friends if she didn't look like such a pig, right? Like, who wants to be seen with her when they go out places? It's like embarrassing and all. I know I would be anyway, I don't know about you guys."

Rebecca had had enough. "Guys, listen to me, she has a very serious medical problem and has to take medication to save her life. The medication saves her life, but it causes her to gain weight. She eats no more food than you or I and she tries to exercise more than we do. She can't help it. We should be her friend and give her support and encouragement, not be her enemies and talk mean and cruel behind her back.

Jaycee cocked her head to one side. "She really can't help it and doesn't eat a lot?"

"NO, she doesn't. She really can't help it."

"Oh man, that's tough. I feel bad I came down so rough and judgmental on her." Jaycee said, furrowing her eyebrows.

Lauren looked down at the table. "I guess my comment was really mean. I shouldn't have said it."

Miranda looked around the table and then stared down at her hands. "I guess I should be more embarrassed at my comment than being embarrassed by being seen with her. I'm awful, I guess."

Jaycee looked across the room. "Hey look, she just came into the lunchroom and is sitting over there alone at the table. Why don't we invite her to sit with us?"

Rebecca smiled and stood up. "That sounds like a great idea!I will go and get her."

She walked over to where Ashley was sitting alone. "Hey, everyone wants you to come and sit with us over there."

Ashley's eyes opened wide. "REALLY, for real? They want me to eat with them?" Well, alright!"

They walked over to the table and sat down. They looked at what Ashley was eating. She was eating a salad with grilled chicken, an apple, carrots, and a bottle of vegetable juice. They looked sheepishly at their own trays. Everyone else was eating pizza, fruit punch, potato chips, and cookies.

"Hi Ashley, how are you? I'm glad you can eat with us. Maybe you can hang out with us after school today because we are all going over to Jaycee's house to go swimming." Lauren said.

Ashley's eyes grew big. "That would be great because swimming is great exercise, thank you very much for inviting me!"

"Yeah, we do a lot of things together and you can join us, it will be fun," Miranda said.

Ashley nodded her head. "That would be so much fun and I would love it and would love to have you guys as friends!"

Rebecca was glad her friends could see the truth behind Ashley's weight and listen to her explanation and were going to include her in their friendship group. Ashley would no longer be an outsider, alone in the world and she was no longer bullied in school since she was friends with the popular girls.

****

Jesus told Rebecca this.

Ashley was able to deal with her weight and accept herself for who she was inside and not judge herself on the outside. She learned to love herself for the wonderful person she was. She got her bachelor's and master's degree and went on to be a mental health counselor and treated children and teens with mental health problems. She helped hundreds of people through the years. She married and had three children, a boy, and two girls, and later on six grandchildren. She lived to be 89 years old.

Then He showed her a different scenario

CHAPTER THREE

"Here comes the fat pig Ashley, feel the ground rumble," Paul said in a loud voice.

Ashley ducked her head low and tried to walk past them. But they formed a wall in front of her, blocking her from going forward.

"How many donuts did you eat this morning, Ashley? Ten dozen? And washed it down with twenty dozen gallons of milk?" Everyone roared with laughter.

Paul grabbed her backpack from her back and spun her around. She lost her footing and fell to the ground.

"EARTHQUAKE!" Braydon yelled at the top of his voice.

Ashley started crying and tears escaped that flowed down her cheeks. She got up from the ground and looked around for her backpack. Paul had it. He started throwing it over her head to Jason and Braydon and they played keep-away with it.

"Please give me back my backpack and please stop being so mean to me. I did nothing to you guys and I just want to be left alone." Her tears were coming fast now and her shoulders were heaving up and down. Snot dripped from her nose and she wiped it on her sleeve.

"Awwwwww, the fat baby is crying, look at her blubbering. Wahhhhh, wahhhhhh, cry, baby, cry.. Look at her snotty nose that she wipes on her sleeve like a two-year-old. That grosses me out, seriously, she is a pig." Jason taunted her, which made her cry even harder.

Jason tossed the backpack, and she managed to grab it and she held it close to her body.

Suddenly, she had dirt on her hair and in her mouth. Paul had picked up a handful of dirt and thrown it at her. She wiped it away and shook out her hair. While she was bent over, she felt a barrage of small pebbles rain over her body and head. She slowly raised herself and felt another volley of rocks across her face and chest. This time, they stung and hurt.

"Ouch. owwww. That hurt!"

Everyone laughed and then Jason threw another handful of dirt and it landed squarely in Ashely's face and hair. She brushed most of it away but some of it was in her mouth, nose, and eyes. She gently rubbed her eyes and experienced the gritty pain of something in it. She ground her teeth and there was a gritty sensation. Just then, the bus came rumbling down the road. The torments stopped for the time being and the kids got on the bus. Ashely was the last one on and she had to squint her eyes to see where she was going. Her eyes stung from the dirt in them. Thankfully there was a seat right behind the bus driver and she sat down. She worked on getting the dirt out of her eyes. They started tearing up with big, hot, tears that washed the dirt away. She had a juice box of apple juice and she used that to wash out the taste and grit of the dirt. She managed to arrive at school with no more torment and abuse.

****

The next day Ashely was jumping rope outside trying to get exercise. She knew she had a medical problem and medicine made her gain weight

She was up to 100 jumps when someone grabbed her jump rope out of her hands. It burned her hands, and she turned around. It was Jason.

"Give me back my jump rope."

"Why? You're gonna cause massive craters in the playground if you keep jumping. You're gonna cause a major earthquake with your massive size by jumping."

"Just give me back my rope."

Jason swung the rope around and it hit her in the legs. "Ouch! That hurt! Stop it and give me back my rope."

Jason kept swinging the rope out of her reach and every so often would snap it at her legs, causing her to shriek.

Paul stood by and watched, and then came in and joined Jason. They wrapped the rope around Ashley and she struggled to get free. "Let me go. Stop this. "She looked around for an adult or anyone who would help but saw none. Finally, the bell rang and the boys took off. Ashley put the rope into her backpack and walked back into the school. She got to her classroom and put her backpack away and went to sit down. Jason sat two desks in front of her and stuck out his foot when she walked by. She tripped and went sprawling to the floor. The teacher looked up.

"What happened Ashley, are you alright?

Ashley stood up and faced the teacher. "Jason stuck his foot out and tripped me."

"Is this true Jason?"

Jason put on an innocent face. "No, I didn't do that. She must have tripped over her own feet."

"That's NOT true, Jason and you know it!" Ashley said with force.

Jason pulled his lips down. "But it is Mrs. Wilson. I really did not trip her."

The teacher had a bias toward the popular kids and gave them special consideration. "Ashley, I'm sure you just thought he tripped you. You must be more careful and watch where you are going."

Ashley's face was crestfallen. Even the teachers sided with the popular kids and didn't give her any consideration. She knew she wasn't going to get any help from her teachers.

****

Have you seen how Ashley was dressed today? It looked like a clown car where they squished too many clowns in and the car burst at its seams." Jaycee said and everyone laughed.

Jaycee was a beautiful girl with golden blonde hair and crystal blue eyes. She had the perfect complexion with nary a blemish or mark.

"I bet she eats a hundred dozen donuts and washes it down with two hundred gallons of soda for breakfast every day. But, really, who eats like that and lets themselves get that fat? REALLY? Who does?" Miranda said.

Miranda was equally beautiful with a thin, lithe body, strawberry blonde hair, and emerald-colored eyes. She also had a perfect creamy white complexion.

Lauren spread her hands out wide. "Why would someone let themselves get that way? I would stop eating and go on a diet and exercise my ass off if I started getting big. And I say STARTED because I would never let myself get that big in the first place."

Lauren was the most beautiful of them all and the most popular girl in school. She had raven black hair that hung down her back in spiral curls and agua blue eyes. Her skin was tanned from tanning beds and it had no blemishes or spots.

"Yeah, she's lazy and a pig and doesn't care what she looks like, so why should we care about being her friend, right guys?" Lauren asked, and held her palms up high.

"I agree," Miranda said. and she slapped Laurens's palm.

"Yeah, for sure! Look she's sitting by herself over by the front." Jaycee said.

"Hey, watch this." And Miranda got up and held a plate filled with green beans, meatloaf, and mashed potatoes with gravy, and walked over to Ashley. She slowed down when she was next to her and then she made herself trip. The plate landed right in Ashley's lap, face down with the food splattering all over Ashley's clothes.

Ashley jumped up. "My clothes! You got your food all over my clothes! I have nothing to change into and my mother has no car to bring me up anything so I have to stay this way all day! You did this on purpose."

Miranda put on a sweet, innocent smile. "But it was an accident, Ashley. It truly was. I tripped over my feet because I'm just so clumsy."

The lunch lady came over." What happened here?"

"She spilled this on me on purpose!" Ashley's face was bright red and her lips were tightly pressed across her teeth.

"What do you say about this Miss Davis?"

Miranda put on her sweetest expression. "I was walking to throw it out. I'm on a diet, you see, and I wanted to get rid of the extra food I didn't want to eat, so I was headed to the garbage can when I tripped over my own two feet. I am embarrassed to say, but I can be clumsy like that. I am so sorry."

"She's lying. She did it on purpose and she's putting on a sweet act for you."

"She seems genuine, Ashley, and she seems to be sorry and contrite. This was an accident, an awful one, but an accident nonetheless, so go to the bathroom and clean yourself up as best as you can."

"That's it? That's all you're gonna do?"

"Ashley, go get cleaned up." And the lunch lady walked away.

The girls at the table bust into laughter and Ashley turned around and faced them. Miranda walked back to the table and turned around, she had a sly grin on her face and she raised her hand and waved at Ashley. Lauren slapped Miranda on the back and threw her head back and laughed so loud everyone in the lunchroom turned and looked. No one looked down on them because they were the "cool" kids. Ashley's face turned beet red, and she ran from the room in tears. She rushed into the bathroom and tried to get as much food off her clothes as she could and she hoped the water dried quickly. Her whole front was soaked and there were brown stains all over her pink shirt and light pink leggings. She wished she had worn darker clothes today, but she had no idea this would happen. The bell had rung by the time she was finished and she walked into the classroom late. Everyone stopped what they were doing and looked at her. The whispering and pointing started and half the class started laughing at her while the other half smirked and gave each other looks. Ashely wanted to run right out of there but she forced herself to take her seat. During class, the person behind her kept kicking her seat. She turned around, and it was Jason. She tried to ignore him but finally, she turned and told him to stop. The teacher heard her.

"Miss Lincoln, do you have something to share with the class?"

"Um, no.... it's just........ he's kicking my chair, and it's bothering me, is all."

"Mr. Stevens, what is your defense?"

"She's lying, I'm not doing it. Why don't you ask the surrounding people? They would have seen me doing it, right?" Jason crossed his hands over his chest.

"That is true Mr. Stevens. So folks, was he kicking Miss Davis's chair?" The teacher cocked his head to one side.

A chorus of no's rang through the room and not one person came to Ashley's defense. She sat there frozen in her seat.

"So, Miss Davis, you are lying. See to it you don't do that again and don't interrupt the class again."

Ashley sat there with cold shivers going up to her spine and her body trembled and her hands shook. The kicking started again, this time with more force. He put his feet on either side of her chair and tried to push her off her seat. She tried to push her desk and chair forward, but then so did he. He leaned forward and grabbed her hair and yanked. She held back a shriek and covered her mouth with her hand. Finally, the bell rang, and she ran outside into the hallway. She looked for a friendly face in the crowds, someone who would reach down inside her and see her heart and not her immense size but there was no one. It had been like that since she was a little girl. They looked at her size and not at her heart and never gave her a fighting chance at friendship. She literally had never had one friend in her entire life. Even adults looked down at her. Her teachers were rude to her and they allowed the other students to be so also and they always took their sides in disputes. She couldn't imagine living the rest of her life this way, being alone and it wasn't what she wanted. She wanted out. She wanted to be free from the pain. She wanted to die. She thought of the different ways she could do it and settled on slitting her wrists. She would do it right here in school. Let them see her pain. Let them deal with the mess that they caused. Let them have the stigma of suicide at their school and maybe the students will feel guilty for how they treated her. She would buy the razor blade today and do it tomorrow.

****

The next day Ashley endured hell at the bus stop but it did not bother her and she actually had a smile on her face. The kids looked at her strangely when she smiled at their torment. It was the same on the bus and in the homeroom. First-period class, she asked to go to the bathroom. She locked herself in the stall. She took out a razor blade and held it over her wrist. She knew you were supposed to slice up and down and not across. She made a few hesitant cuts and finally made the first deep cut. An artery was hit because the blood spurted up and hit her face. It dripped down into the toilet. She made a cut on the other wrist, even deeper. Afterward, she took the slippery razor blade and made an even deeper cut into the first wrist. She laid back as her blood poured into the toilet. For added measure, she had taken large quantities of aspirin yesterday and this morning to help her blood not clot and come out stronger. It took fifteen minutes for her to die and another half an hour for her teacher to realize she was gone from class and the bathroom was checked. A maintenance man opened up the stall and the teacher and nurse screamed. Ashely was sitting there slumped over, lifeless and pale with her lap covered in blood and sitting over a toilet that was filled with her blood. A coroner and the police were called. Curious teens stood outside the bathroom and teachers tried to shoo them away. But they were there when they brought Ashley out in the body bag. Jason, Braydon, Paul, Miranda, Jaycee, Lauren, and the rest watched in stunned horror as the stretcher passed by them. Paul made a comment about her needing a specially made extra-large coffin but Braydon slapped him in the head for saying it, and the others glared at him. They had somber looks on their faces as Ashley passed by in the body bag.

****

Rebecca watched the scene in horror and then slowly realized she had a part in keeping Ashley alive and having a good and happy life. She never knew this was what would have happened if she had never stuck up for Ashley and befriended her and stopped the abuse from other kids.

Then another scene flashed before Rebecca.

CHAPTER FOUR

S andy was writing in her journal and it was her favorite time of day. She was a natural-born writer and would write for hours at a time. She poured her heart into her writing and wanted to be a freelance writer, book author, and editor when she graduated college. She was going to Broadhaven University and getting her bachelor's degree in Communications with an emphasis on Writing. She had many goals and aspirations but she also had a dark side too. She was diagnosed with several mental illnesses when she was 13 and spent a lot of time in hospital and special schools. No one thought she would ever make it to college. She only got in because of the EOP program. This is for people who don't qualify for college because of various reasons. Sandy's mental health reasons qualified her for the program. She still struggled daily with symptoms of the diseases and the side effects of the medications. She was diagnosed with Bipolar 1 and Schizoaffective Disorder and also PTSD and to top those off ADHD. She was on antipsychotics, antidepressants, mood stabilizers, and antianxiety medication. Her daily load of pills was heavy. She sometimes felt like she couldn't get through the day. One day she was down and barely could get out of bed and another day she was flying and nothing could stop her and she would go days without sleep. Even with medication, her symptoms were pervasive, but they were unmanageable without medication. She had trouble making friends with her sometimes erratic behavior and loneliness made everything worse. Today, she was ready to give up on everything and she was in a deep funk and depression. She decided to go for a walk. She walked across the campus to the common area and over to where there were flower gardens. It was vacant. She started crying and buried her face in her hands. She didn't hear the person approach her.

"Hey, what's the matter? Are you O. K? My name's Rebecca."

Sandy jumped and looked up. There was a girl standing there, and she reached out and squeezed Sandy's shoulder. She had the kindest eyes Sandy had ever seen, and she trusted her right away.

"Oh, hi. I'm just down in the dumps and depressed and it's making me struggle."

Rebecca sat down next to her. 'Tell me more. I'm willing to listen to you."

Sandy decided to trust Rebecca, and she unburdened her whole past on her. She told her about her mental illnesses and her hospitalizations and her medications.

"I feel like I can't make it through this week with midterms and all that. I have no friends and no one to talk to," "

Rebecca cocked her head to one side. "You need to take it one day at a time. Focus on what you need to do just for today. I'm willing to be your friend. We can be accountability partners for each other. What dorm are you in?"

Sandy smiled through her tears. "I am in Grant Dorm."

Rebecca clapped her hands. "REALLY? So am I! I am surprised I haven't seen you before in the dorm but I've seen you in class. I think we are in Math and History together.

Sandy looked sheepish. "I don't come out of my room very much and I am on the first floor by the exit. And yes, I remember you from class but I say as little as possible in class and I try to sit in the back and hide."

Rebecca smiled. "That's O. K. You can work on that. You need to develop self-confidence and you need to have someone believe in you. It's almost dinnertime, let's go to the cafeteria and get something to eat."

So they wandered over to the Food Hall and ate dinner and talked about their pasts and childhoods. When they finished, they exchanged cell phone numbers.

"I will call you tomorrow morning and I will see you in class at 11:00, we can sit together. Try to have a good night and sleep well." Rebecca said as she gave Sandy a hug.

****

Rebecca did as she promised and called Sandy.

"Hey girl, how are you this morning?"

"Hi, Rebecca. You remembered to call me."

"Of course I did, I said I would and you will find that I always keep my word. Are you up and dressed yet and had breakfast?'

There was some silence on the phone. "Um, no, I'm still in my pajamas and haven't eaten."

"O. K, get dressed, there's still some time to eat before class. You want to eat breakfast to give you energy for the day or you will be dragging. Meet me at the Food Hall in twenty minutes."

"Um, O. K, I can do that."

So, twenty minutes later Sandy was standing in front of the food court when Rebecca came ambling along. She smiled when she saw Sandy standing there waiting for her. They walked in, grabbed their trays, and got in line. After they grabbed their food, they wandered around a bit and found a table by a window, and sat down.

"So, how are you feeling today?" Rebecca asked.

Sandy looked down at her food. "I didn't want to get up this morning."

Rebecca rubbed her hand. "But you did, didn't you? That's what counts."

Sandy looked up and smiled. "Yeah, I guess you're right."

"I am! Just doing what we don't want to do is a victory no matter how small it is. Now, we better hurry, we have History and Mr. Abrams is a stickler for being on time."

They picked up their trays, dumped their garbage, and walked out of the hall into the sunlight. Their next class was in a building a short walk away and they managed to get there in a few minutes and were on time.

Later that evening, they got together to study for a Math test they were having the next day. Sandy was convinced she was going to fail because she couldn't grasp certain concepts and she was too shy and ashamed to ask for help. She was already close to failing the class and if she failed this test and the mid-term, she would fail the class and need to take it over. So they sat and poured over the book and practiced problem after problem until a light went on in Sandy's head and she grasped the concepts of the math.

"I think I really understand now. It all makes sense the way you explained it to me and the way we kept going over it repeatedly. I've got an idea that I am going to pass this test!" Sandy raised her fist in the air.

Rebecca nodded her head and smiled. "I'm sure you will and I have confidence in you. Just remember what we talked about and remember the formulas and you will get the problems correct. Let's call it a night, it's 11:00."

They said goodnight and Sandy left for her room excited about tomorrow.

****

The day after the tests, the grades were reported and Rebecca and Sandy lined up to see their grades. Rebecca got a 98% and much to Sandy's surprise and delight, she got a 94%. That was going to help her grades immensely.

Sandy walked back to her room in a great mood. But it didn't last long after she got a phone call from her mother. She was so excited to tell her mom about her grade and she expected her to be excited. But her mom told her that was what she should have been getting all along and that was what she expected of her. No excitement and no praise. She should've known this would be her mother's reaction. Her mother expected so much from her and she had been nothing but a disappointment through the years. You would think that if she met her expectations with a grade of 94% that she would be happy, but no, it was just more expectations. She hung up the phone and curled up in a ball on her bed. She felt a blanket of depression envelop her and she had a strong desire to cut herself. She got up and walked to her desk. Her roommate was sitting at her desk. There were razor blades stashed there, and she grabbed one and then climbed back on her bed, which was the top bunk. She laid on her side and raised up her shirt, which showed a stomach covered with scars. She drew the razor over her skin and a bright red line appeared. Satisfied, she did it three more times, and then she got down and put the razor away. She wondered if she would tell Rebecca about this. She wanted to stay in bed the rest of the day and skip her afternoon class and she closed her eyes and fell asleep. There was a knock on the door and her roommate answered it. It was Rebecca.

"Hey girl, you're gonna be late for your class. I tried texting you but you haven't been responding. Come on, we can talk on the way." She grabbed Sandy's hand and her books and they rushed out of the room.

"I told my mom about my grade and instead of excitement, she told me it was what she expected me to get and what I should've been doing all along. It made me depressed. It made me do something else too. I cut."

Rebecca stopped. "You cut?"

Sandy looked sheepish and raised her shirt to show her stomach. "Yeah, I've done it for a long time." Then she lowered her shirt.

Rebecca grabbed her arm and hurried her along. "We have to make a pact about that. If you feel like doing it, you have to contact me. Any time and any day, you call me. You got it? Will you make a pact with me that you will not do it without talking to me first?" She glanced over at her.

Sandy nodded. "Yes, I can do that. I never had someone do that for me before."

"O. K. Then it's a plan."

They got to class just in time for the teacher to take attendance and they found their seats and sat down.

****

Sandy passed that semester with flying colors and moved on to the next semester. She wasn't looking forward to some of her classes. One class, in particular, she was dreading, and that was Public Speaking. The thought of speaking in front of a group of people made her bowels loose and her stomach recoil. She tried to get the class dropped and changed but could not. Her academic adviser could not help her even though she begged her. She was told she needed to take this course to get her degree. This threw her into a deep depression that even Rebecca had a hard time bringing her out of. The first time she had to get up in class, she spent twenty minutes in the bathroom throwing up and had to ask to go to the nurse's office and give her speech another day. The next day it was planned, she stayed in bed and refused to get out, and missed the class. The same thing happened the next time. Finally, the teacher told her she was going to fail the course if she missed again and Rebecca thought some tough love was needed.

"Sandy, you got this. No one is going to laugh at you. They are all just as nervous as you are the first time. Very few people are natural-born public speakers. They are far and few between and I know I am not one of them either. I get nervous speaking in front of groups too. I stand up there and focus on what I need to say and I think about the fact that I am a capable person and I got this. And I know YOU got this, Sandy. Don't expect perfection the first time. Just get up and do it and then get down. Get it over with and it will be done and you won't need to worry about it anymore."

Sandy looked skeptical. "I don't know."

Rebecca patted her on the back. "You got this!"

Sandy walked to the auditorium and sat down. She felt cold shivers down her spine and her stomach was recoiling. She took some slow, deep breaths and let them out slowly. Then her name was called. She hesitated for a minute and then thought of what Rebecca said to her and slowly got out of her seat. She walked up to the podium and placed her papers on it. She adjusted the microphone and then looked out at her fellow students. They were all smiling encouragingly at her. Then she started to speak and spoke the whole fifteen minutes she was allotted and when she was finished, she couldn't believe she had done it. She was so proud of herself and it wasn't half as bad as she thought it was going to be. She experienced some new confidence build inside her that wasn't there before. When the class was over, she got on the phone and called Rebecca.

"I did it! And I think I did it well. I talked the whole allotted time, I made eye contact, I didn't stutter, and I didn't look at the papers too much. I didn't vomit all over the stage!"

"That's awesome. Especially the last one." And Rebecca laughed at that. "I knew you could do it. I had confidence in you! I'm proud of you! Well done, Sandy, well done!"

****

Sandy had read about a girl who was raped on campus. There wasn't the outrage she thought there should be. She went on the computer and researched it further and found out there had been 12 cases in the past three years and she was stunned. Where was the outrage? Where was the picketing for reform? She experienced such a response because she had been sexually abused by a family member as a child and knew the damage it caused. She understood it exasperated her mental health symptoms and made her the shy, timid person she was. She met Rebecca at the gardens,

"Hey, Rebecca. Did you hear about the girl who was raped a few days ago?"

Rebecca frowned. "No, I did not. That's awful. Did they catch the person?"

Sandy tugged at her hair. "Yes, and they want to try it before the student court and not the police. How the heck is that even possible?"

Rebecca cocked her head to one side. "I don't know. I've heard of that done and colleges trying to sweep it under the rug."

Sandy slapped her knee with her hand. "But they HAVE swept it under the rug. There've been twelve rapes and assaults in just the last three years on this campus alone. And there's no outrage or anything."

Rebecca stared at Sandy and narrowed her eyes. "Then YOU start the outrage. YOU start the picketing, start a petition that says the police have to handle all these cases. Start an organization."

Sandy widened her eyes. "I do that? I couldn't be the one to start something and be in charge. I'm scared of my own shadow. And you know how I am with public speaking."

Rebecca smiled. "I know you gave a speech and overcame your fear and did a great job and got an A on it. Am I correct?"

Sandy looked sheepish. "Yeah, I know. Do you really think I could start something? Would people actually follow me?"

"You will never know unless you try, and I will be your biggest supporter!" Rebecca reached over and gave her a hug.

****

Sandy looked over the group of students that was assembled before her and her forehead started sweating. She had printed out petitions to make it mandatory for rapes and assaults to be reported to the police instead of the campus police and with the student court handling it. And she planned a picket in front of the administration building. She had called the local news station to tell them what she was doing, and she had hoped there would be a good turnout. She had printed out flyers and passed them out on campus and put them up on bulletin boards. To her immense astonishment, over 250 students had arrived. She looked out over the group and there were women and men and they all looked excited. The time came, and she took a big, deep breath and slowly let it out, and then stood before the group with a bullhorn she had borrowed from an instructor.

"Hello, I am so glad you took the time to come out today for such a good cause. The time has come to end rape and assault cases being handled by the school. The time has come for them to be reported to the police where they belong."

After she said that, everyone cheered loudly and clapped their hands. She looked over to the side and saw TV cameras and realized the news station had arrived. There were two other photographers taking pictures, and she assumed they were from the newspapers she had also contacted.

"We need to demand that this be done and we need to demand more safety measures be taken. Twelve rape and assault cases have been reported in the last three years. ONE case is too many!"

Again, the cheers filled the area and everyone clapped their hands.

Her fear and anxiety were leaving, and she experienced her confidence soar.

"We will keep petitioning and we will keep gathering to show them we are serious about this. And hopefully, our numbers will grow and the college will be forced to change its policies. Whether because they want to or because they are being shamed or because they are forced to!"

There were more cheers and applause.

"Now we will have several brave women who will share their stories of being attacked to show why we need to do this and why this is so incredibly important. This will put a human face on our cause."

Then she had four women come forward and share their stories of rape and assault on campus.

She ended the protest by having everyone shout "No More" repeatedly for five minutes and then it was over.

Rebecca came up to her and gave her a big hug. "I'm so proud of you. You did amazing, and you were a true leader and you inspired me and everyone else here."

****

Three months later, the semester was almost over and Sandy was doing great. She had a GPA of 3.6, better than she ever thought possible. Then today she got the best news ever. The college board had met, and it was decided that all rapes and assaults would be reported to the local police and would not be handled internally by the college. They also will hire more security to patrol the campus, especially at night and they are installing cameras that will be monitored by security 24 hours a day. She raced through the campus to get to her dorm to find Rebecca. She pounded on her door and she heard her call her in.

"Rebecca, guess what?"

Rebecca smiled. "What's up? You look excited."

"The college decided they will report all rapes and assaults to the police, they are installing cameras that will be monitored 24 hours a day and they are hiring more security at night to patrol and it only took three months. We had four rallies and four petitions and we had the phone call marathon."

Rebecca stood up and hugged her. "See, I told you that you could do anything if you put your mind to it, and you did. I'm so proud of you! This is a big accomplishment and you do not know just how many women you'll have helped now and in the future. You have left a huge stamp on this college and people's lives."

Sandy stared at Rebecca and cocked her head to the side. "Yeah, but you know what? I never would have done it if it weren't for YOU encouraging me! This stamp on the college is yours too and don't try to deny it, Rebecca!"

Rebecca just smiled and said nothing.

****

Eighteen months later, Sandy was meeting with thirty people from twenty-five other colleges. They were going to set up a rally and a campaign to get their colleges to also report rapes and assaults on campus to the local police and improve the security provided by the college. The movement was spreading, and she had heard from a total of forty colleges across the states that also wanted to do the same. And she had twenty-five people who had already done these things on their own twenty compasses and drastically lowered the rate of rapes and assaults each year, some down to zero. The campaign became known as "Take Back the Night." They were here for a meeting. Sandy was going to get the shock of her life.

"Sandy, we would like you to be president of the national organization. The way you have formed this movement from just a handful of colleges to almost half the colleges in the northeast in such a short time is nothing short of amazing and you haven't stopped. This is growing as we speak. You've shown you have the leadership skills needed for the position. Will you accept?" Debbie asked.

Debbie was going to be president of the New York State chapter. She was a short woman, slightly overweight but with a huge personality. .

Sandy turned bright red and squirmed in her chair. "I don't know what to say. I don't feel qualified."

Jessie puts her hands in front of her. "What more do you need to do to be qualified, Sandy? You've done more than any of us here. You ARE the most qualified."

Jessi was going to be the vice president of the national organization. She was a tall woman with vibrant red hair that hung down her back in springy spiral curls. Her magnetic smile came from thick full lips.

Sandy looked out at all the faces staring expectantly at her. She smiled and nodded her head. "I accept." She looked toward the back of the room and saw Rebecca. Their eyes met, and they smiled at each other and Rebecca gave her the thumbs-up sign.

****

Before long, it was graduation time and Sandy was getting her gown on. She stood before a floor-length mirror and tears came to her eyes. She put on the gold sash that signified that she was graduating magna cum laude and slowly ran her hands down over it. Her GPA was 3.9. She never thought she would see this day much less graduate with such honors. She had not had a hospitalization in four and a half years. She was president of a national organization to prevent rape and assault on college campuses and she was making a huge difference in probably millions of women's lives. *Yes, she thought, wow, millions.* She was accepted into a Master's degree program at this college and she found a job as a writer for a regional magazine. She wrote and self-published four books on Amazon Kindle Publishing and has sold over 29,000 copies. One book was about overcoming mental illness and the fact that mental illness is a part of you but it is not WHO you are. She got to speak on several podcasts about the book and was featured in the local paper and on the local news station. That book sold over 14,000 copies and is still selling copies each day. Her mother finally had to give her praise and credit for her accomplishments. She left the dorm room and walked out to the field where the ceremony was going to be held. She saw Rebecca up ahead. They both got in line. They hugged each other and then the music came on and Sandy walked into the field to her seat. She sat through the speeches and soon she heard her name called and she walked up to the stage. She took her diploma and turned, and smiled for the pictures.

****

Sandy went on to get her Master's Degree in Communications and Writing and got a job as a journalist for a news station. She met her husband and had five children, two boys, and three girls. They moved on to achieve successful careers and gave her twelve grandchildren. She remained president of the Take Back The Night Coalition until she was 40 years old and then passed the banner to the younger generation. She volunteered at the local rape crisis hotline and crisis center and she became a peer counselor at her local mental health club. She retired at age 65 and died peacefully at home surrounded by her family at age 86.

****

Jesus turned to Rebecca. "And if it weren't for you, would she had done all that?"

Rebecca looked at him. "I don't know."

Jesus smiled sadly at her. "I guess we shall see."

CHAPTER FIVE

Sandy was shocked she got into college because her high school transcript was less than desirable. She had a 2.8 GPA and wasn't in any clubs or organizations and didn't do any volunteer work. She didn't take any advanced placement courses or even any honors courses. She applied to the college just for the heck of it and applied for the EOP, Education Opportunity Program. That program helps high school kids with less than desirable transcripts and who come from disadvantaged backgrounds get into colleges when they otherwise would not be eligible or be desirable by the college. She applied and shared that she had several mental health diagnoses and spent a lot of time in hospitals and special schools during her high school years and it got her into the program. She had to attend special meetings and groups the program had and also undergo tutoring. She also had to keep her GPA over 2.5. She thought that was not a bad compromise when she would have been stuck at a community college, otherwise. Not that community colleges were bad, but they weren't real colleges. For example, her local community college did not have dorms and she wanted to get out of her home and live in a college dorm which made it seem more like real college life. She also wanted to go straight for her Bachelor's degree and not have to get her Associates' degree first. She was going for her degree in Communications with a concentration in writing. Sandy was a writer. She wrote for hours in her journal and poured her heart out in them when she had no one to talk to, which was quite often. She wanted to write a book and be an author but even with her copious writing, she never had the confidence to get started. She struggled with her mental health problems and today she was in a funk. She had only gotten halfway through the semester and already she was struggling. Her grades were abysmal and coming close to being put on academic probation. She received tutoring through the EOP program but her motivation level just wasn't at the level it needed to be to get successful grades in college. She decided to take a walk and ended up in the flower gardens. She broke down and started crying and put her face in her hands. Her shoulders shook up and down and her nose ran. She wanted to give up and just leave the college, even though it was a miracle she got in. She was at her wit's end with her depression and anxiety. All she wanted to do was curl up in a ball in her bed and pull the covers over her head. She stayed there for an hour then dragged herself back to her dorm and got her books for her English class. It was a writing class and she should be excited about it. It was what she loved to do but even that couldn't light a flame under her. She wandered over to the building where her class was and walked in. She found her classroom and took a seat in the last row in the back. The other students came pouring in and soon the instructor was standing before the class.

"Did you guys write your papers on The Giver? I am going to call on you and I want you to give a synopsis on your paper before you hand it in."

Sandy froze. Speaking in class was one of her extreme phobias. Public speaking terrified her, and she was not good in social situations. She would rather be alone and talk to people through her keyboard, anonymous and safe. One by one the students got up and gave their synopsis and soon it was the person right before Sandy, a beautiful, popular girl, who seemed to have it all. Her name was Amanda Graves.

Amanda stood up and flipped her golden blond hair over her shoulder and put on a pouty smile. "The society in this story is a Utopia. In the book, society is hidden from a lot of things that are "imperfect". The social aspect of this book is flabbergasting. In the book, Jonas is presented with two ideas on a moral or just society. The first one is obviously the utopia he's grown up in, and the second is a society like ours, which the giver shows him through memories. When Jonas really hits a climax in which society makes more sense is after he finds out what love is. After he has a memory of love given to him by the Giver, he goes home to ask his father if he loves him. When his father says no, he doesn't love him but just enjoys his presence, Jonas's mind is set. He is frustrated with the fact that nobody else around him understands him and no one knows or can know the things he knows. Throughout the book, there is a strong message about society and how different it is from ours today. Reading something from the perspective of a different social layout is very interesting but at times also very frustrating. Things we think are moral and fair are often overlooked in the book and at times you feel for the character as he is angered and upset over things he once looked at as okay." She flipped her hair back and gave a wide grin, and sat down.

The teacher nodded and smiled. "Very good Amanda, very good. I liked that, and it was original."

Sandy experienced her whole body trembling. She knew she couldn't give a synopsis as well as that or as long. She stood up on legs that were like jelly. "Um, The Giver is a dystopian... um, story where things are...... um... perfect to the....um visible eye but...... um down under there are dark.... um things...... Words are used that mean one thing but actually....... um means another like Newspeak in Orwell's novel... One example is the word...

um.... Release which is um.... actually... death and murder..... When Jonah finds out.... um, the truth.... um, he has to... um decide if he... is... going to... um...... go with the... status quo or fight back... um against the system." Then she sat down and the sweat dripped down her back.

The teacher stared at her for a moment and nodded his head. "O. K, now that we have finished that please hand in your papers to the front."

Sandy's face grew hot and red. The teacher did not even acknowledge what she said. He did for everyone else in the class but her. *My verbal synopsis must have been the worst in the class, she thought.* She hoped her paper was at least better than what she just said. She wondered if they were going to get graded on what they had to stand up and say but he wrote nothing down, so she doubted he was going to do that, which was a relief. She was anxious to get out of there and watched the clock tick by. Finally, the forty-five-minute class was over and she picked up her books and rushed out the door. She headed to her dorm where she planned on holding up for the rest of the day until her 1:00, forty-five-minute math class and then into the evening. But she ran into her math instructor.

"Hello, Sandy. How are you?"

Sandy tried to smile. "I'm O. K."

Her teacher cocked her head to one side. "Are you ready for the test tomorrow? Your average is almost failing so if you fail this test or get below a 70, you are going to fail for the semester."

Sandy's face turned beet red. "I'm having... um... a hard time... um... understanding Algebra... um... Basic.... math I am fine... with but once I get to... um..... Algebra, I get stuck.

"Have you availed yourself a tutor? This is remedial math, Sandy. It's not even a credit course and you have to pass it to get into the actual Algebra course, which naturally, is much harder."

Sandy looked down at the floor for a moment, and then looked up with tears in her eyes. "I have a tutor... um.... through the EOP program. But she is not... um... patient......... and if I don't understand something... um... right away,...... she moves on to something else...... um.... It's not helping....... anything at all."

The teacher made a wry face. "Well, it IS frustrating and I understand where she is coming from. This is math you should have learned in high school. This is college now. No one is supposed to be holding your hand here. You are an adult. You should have sought out another tutor then and I am not sure why you have not done so if you think this tutor is not working. It's a little late now to do anything about this test. You will have to take the course over again. Possibly next time you will be a responsible adult and get help at the beginning. Well, it is what it is. I will see you later."

She left Sandy crying and Sandy watched her leave and wondered why the teacher was so mean. She did not even acknowledge her tears and sadness. *Maybe she is right and I should have done that. I dropped the ball again in my life and now will have to face the consequences, she thought.*

When the time came for her math class, she hurried down the path that led to the building where the class was held. She was running late and did not watch the clock or set an alarm. She arrived at the building and entered it, and went down the hall to the classroom. She was ten minutes late, and she opened the door, everyone was in their seats and the teacher was standing before the class.

"Nice of you to drop in Sandy. Did you forget the time of the class? Sit down in your seat and we will start the test."

Sandy's face grew hot and red and she had perspiration beads dotting her forehead. She thought the eyes of the other students were on her when she made her way to her seat. There was an empty one in the back row, which was her favorite seat. The teacher handed out the test, and Sandy stared at it for a while. In the first question, she had some idea of how to do it. But the second one she had no clue about. She basically guessed where she had to show her work, she left a question mark. She understood right away she failed the test. There was no doubt about it. Sandy got up and walked to the teacher's desk and made eye contact and she gave her a wistful smile. The teacher just raised her eyebrows and compressed her lips when Sandy tried to smile at her. *She doesn't like me at all, thought Sandy. No one likes me here, no one at all.* She rushed out of the room, down the hall, and out the door. She got to her dorm and saw a group of girls gathered by the entranceway. They were laughing and talking and looked like they were lots of fun. She approached the door timidly, and they made room for her to pass. She tried to make eye contact with one of them in hope of possibly an introduction. But they continued their banter around her as she moved past them and through the door. No one said hi or even acknowledged her presence except to move out of her way. She wandered into her room and plopped down on her bed, laid down, and curled up in the fetal position. She stayed that way until morning only getting up to go to the bathroom.

****

Two days later she realized she had missed all her classes yesterday by staying in bed. Today she was going to find out what she got on her math test. She needed at least an 85 to pass the course for the semester and she highly doubted she had done that. She rolled out of bed and stood up, then she stretched her taut, aching muscles. She had a burning sensation in her stomach and she was a little lightheaded. She wasn't able to remember the last time she ate a meal or drank water. She didn't bother taking a shower even though she obviously needed it and she dashed out of the dorm and down to the Dining Hall. It was 8:05 and there were a few other students already there. She got in line and ordered French toast and syrup and got two cups of orange juice and then took her tray and sat down. There were several tables with empty spots next to other people but as she approached them, no one gave her more than a glance. No welcoming and inviting smiles of invitation to sit were offered, so she walked to the back of the room to an empty table, sat, and ate alone. When she was finished, she strolled to her next class. She wasn't late and got there five minutes early. It was her writing class. She was getting back her paper today. She thought she was a good writer, and she had written things her whole childhood and adolescence, even short stories she jotted down in notebooks. In high school, she had gotten good grades on all her papers and essays but that was in her special schools and hospitals. This wasn't the first paper this semester, in fact, it was the fourth and the last one. She had gotten a B, C, and a C+ on the other ones and she had a B- average in the class right now. *This paper will determine if I still have that, she thought. And I can lose it in an instant.* She arrived at the classroom and took her seat. The other students came wandering in and soon the class started. The teacher started handing out the papers and she placed Sandy's on her desk before her upside down. Sandy took a deep breath and turned the paper over, and gasped. She had gotten a D. A freaken, lousy, awful D. The teacher had written on the paper that her paper had no depth, no characterization, and no personal voice. It was bland and generic and uninteresting to the reader. And he said her oral presentation was awful. *OUCH, that stings, she thought.* He really laid it hard on me and it means my final grade in the class will be a C-. She really needed this class to bolster her GPA, which was suffering greatly. If she went below a 2.5 GPA, she could be kicked out of college. In five days she will find out. if her nerves didn't kill her first. If she failed at this, her mother would tell her, "I told you so". She didn't think Sandy should go away to college and didn't want her to go. Her father didn't care one way or the other. Only her grandma had faith in her and was cheering her on. The rest of her family also did not have faith in her and was surprised she was going away to college. They knew her struggles in adolescence and didn't think she would handle them well. *I guess one cheerleader is better than none, she thought.* Soon that class was over and she headed to the Dining Hall and ate. Once again, she ate alone. She was halfway through lunch when she got a surprise, someone propped a tray down at her table across from her. The girl was at least six feet tall and thin and willowy like a reed. Her cheekbones were prominent, and she had thick, pouty lips. Her hair was jet black and hung straight down her back to her waist. Her clothes were all black, Goth-like, as was her black eyeliner and black lipstick. She sat there for a few minutes in silence and then spoke up.

"Hey. My name is Ruby, what's yours/"

Startled by her voice, Sandy responded. "Um, my name is Sandy."

"Cool. How are you doing in school? I see you around but mostly alone." Ruby said as she continued to eat her lunch.

Sandy was surprised she was noticed. "I am not doing well. And yeah, I don't have any friends."

Ruby nodded. "Yeah, I thought so. I have a few friends and we are in a group. I am sure you can tell I'm into Goth."

Sandy looked at her and nodded, and she finished the last bite of her food. "Yeah, of course, I can "

"I'm sure you wouldn't be into us but you can hang out with us occasionally. I also wanted to share something with you. Something that will help you with school, something that will make you more outgoing."

Sandy was intrigued and raised her eyebrows. "Of course, I'd be interested in that."

Ruby pulled something out of her pocket. It was a baggy with some capsules in it. "I have Adderall. It's amazing and I get it cheap. I only charge $2 a capsule. You would start by taking 1 day and work your way up to 3- to 4 a day. I have access to massive amounts of it."

Sandy looked in her pocketbook. She had money. Her grandma was rich and gave her a huge allowance every month, most of which she did not spend and it was building up in her account. "How many do you have right now?"

"I have 50."

Sandy pulled out five twenties from her wallet and handed it to Ruby who discreetly passed her a bigger baggy filled with capsules.

"When you need more, come back to me. I also have other stuff like pot, some E, and some other stuff. You might need pot to come down from the Adderall sometimes to sleep. I have some now if you want. It's $60 a baggy and I have a bowl I can give you." Ruby rummaged in her backpack.

Sandy thought about it and it made sense to her to buy some pot. She rustled through her wallet and pulled out three more twenties. That meant she would need to go to the ATM because she only had $15 left. She handed the money to Ruby and Ruby pulled her pocketbook over and discreetly put the bag of pot and the bowl into it. Then she smiled, jotted down her cell phone number, and then left.

Sandy looked into her pocketbook at the drugs that were in there. She opened the bag of capsules and pulled two out. Ruby said to start with one but she really needed something bad. *I need the extra jolt for my body to respond, she thought.* She popped them in her mouth and drank some of her juice and swallowed them. She was anxious to experience the results. Thirty minutes later her head started to buzz and her nerves were like they were on fire. She had energy like she never had before. Her concentration was amazing, and she was on top of the world. But she was playing with fire. Those with Bipolar 1 should NEVER take Amphetamines like Adderall, EVER. And Sandy knew this and yet, she still did it. She decided to go for a walk and walked close to three miles. When she got back, her muscles were on fire but she wasn't tired. She had her math class to go to, and she tottered over to the class and walked in, and sat down. She did not have any fear of the teacher today and she did not care if the teacher liked her or not. She had trouble sitting through the class and squirmed in her seat. She was able to pay attention, but they were still going over all the material from the class for the final. Then it was time for the final and Sandy sat before the test and got the case of the giggles. It was all she could do to keep from laughing. She wrote down silly answers to the questions on the test. She was sure the teacher would not find them amusing. But she did not care right now. She was the first to finish, and she stood up and brought the test to the desk and laid it down. The teacher looked at her and raised her eyebrows. Sandy shrugged her shoulders and left the room. She practically bounced down the path to her dorm. She bounded into her room and cleaned it up a bit, and then took a shower. She went for another walk and ended up walking close to five miles. She got back to the dorm at 9:00 at night. She was not tired and went online and surfed the internet all night long. Soon, her alarm rang at 7:00 and she glanced over at it, a little shocked. *I've been up all night and I'm not the least bit tired. This is amazing, she thought. It reminds me of when I am manic.* She took more of the Adderall when she felt it start to wear off. Today she would find out her GPA and if she was continuing school this coming Summer Semester. She logged into the student portal and into her college email. And there it was, her grades. For Math, she got an F. For Creative Writing 101, she got a C-. For History, she got a C-, for College Prep, she got a B-. Her GPA was 2.7. She squeaked by, by .2 points and will be staying in school. She was going to the summer session to try to take the math course again.

****

Sandy was sitting in her summer school math class. Her body was shaking, her brain buzzed and her mind was clouded from lack of sleep. She was taking up to six Adderall a day, and she smoked the pot at night and while it relaxed her, it rarely helped her with sleep. She started hearing voices that were not there. Auditory hallucinations were a side effect of amphetamines on a Bipolar 1 person. The voices clouded her thoughts with their incessant shouting and incessant soft whispering in her ears. She also experienced the sensation of someone watching her and being followed. The feeling made her want to crawl out of her skin. Many times during the day, she looked over her shoulder, expecting someone to be following her or to be standing there waiting to get her. Her closet became an ominous cavern a night, and she waited for the door to open and someone or something evil to come out. She bought a night light because she couldn't tolerate the darkness anymore or the shadows that seemed to morph into people or creatures that were increasingly frightening. She could not leave her dorm at night because of the dark and she missed a few EOP programs she was supposed to attend because they ended after 9:00 at night. She told the director she was having mental health problems, and she was honest about being fearful of the dark and of the night and he seemed to accept that as an excuse.

She was failing the math class again even though she had an EOP tutor and an outside tutor that worked with her four times a week. Each one worked with her two nights a week. Sandy just couldn't get it no matter how much she tried. They seemed to think they can explain it in lofty terms and in quick ways that she can't keep up with. *If they would only slow down, she thought. If only I had someone who took their time and explained it to me on my level.* But she couldn't find that person. So several days after summer school ended she logged into her portal and found her grades. She had failed the course again. Thankfully, she had a different teacher. She signed up for next semester's classes and she was taking the remedial math course again, Psychology 101, Public Speaking, Communications 101, and Intermediate Creative Writing 102. She tried to get out of Public Speaking but was told it was a requirement for the degree. This was a nightmare for her beyond her imagination and what she thought she could endure.

She started her classes and increased her Adderall, her anxiety was so out of control and her hallucinations were becoming debilitating. She tried to stop the Adderall and her body crashed and she wasn't able to get out of her bed. She called Ruby to ask her for help.

"Hello?"

"Ruby, oh Ruby, I need your help. I can't sleep. I am hallucinating, I feel like I am gonna jump out of my skin, I tried stopping and I couldn't get out of bed. I need help to feel good."

Ruby was silent for a moment and Sandy thought she hung up. "There is something you can try. It'll make you feel so very wonderful..."

Sandy didn't let Ruby finish. "Whatever it is, bring it over to my dorm room right now. As fast as you can. O. K?"

Ruby laughed and then got serious. "O.K, I'll be right over."

Ten minutes later Ruby was knocking on her dorm room door. Sandy jumped up and let her in.

'What's this stuff that's so great that will make me feel so wonderful?'

"Hold your horse and I'll get it out." She rummaged through her backpack and brought out a big bag filled with smaller packets of white powder. She took one of the smaller packets out. "This is coke. You spread it out on a smooth surface like this and make them into two lines." She showed her how to do it. "Then you take a dollar bill and roll it up like this. And you put it over the lines and you snort it in as hard as you can." And then she did. After she wiped her nose and her eyes were watering. Then she got a big smile on her face. "I feel so very wonderful, let me tell you! Now you try. This first dose is on me."

Sandy lined the powder up in two lines and then rolled the dollar up. She put it over the first line of powder and then snorted it in as hard as she was able to. It burned her nose, and she jerked her head back. Her eyes started watering, and she rubbed her nose. Then she leaned over and did the other line. She sat up and within seconds, her eyes got wide and she put her head back and moaned.

"This is awesome. Oh, my word. This is truly a wonderful experience, one of the best in the world. How long does it last?"

Ruby folded her hands together. "It lasts 4-6 hours depending on your body."

"How much is this?"

Ruby moved her clasped hands up to her chin. " $10 a bag or you can buy a gram for $150, which works out to be cheaper in the long run. But before you decide, I want you to try two other things. I also have meth and crack. Let's hang out and wait for the coke to wear off."

"Do they make you have an even better experience?" Sandy got up and put the TV on.

"You bet they do."

They watched TV for three hours and then Ruby rummaged through her backpack again and brought out another bag that had small bags in it and took one out. She also pulled a small glass tube out. She motioned for Sandy to get closer and she put the white powder in the glass tube and lit it with a lighter. "Breath this in." She instructed Sandy. "Take a deep breath in." Sandy sucked on the tube and breathed in the white vapor from the glass tube and then sat back. She immediately got a huge smile on her face and her head rocked back and forth. "Oh yeah, Oh yeah, this is amazing, this feels so amazing. ahhhhhhh."

"I figured you'd like that the best. We won't even try the crack. This is $5 a bag. And I can give you a gram for $30 and that's four hits. So if you do four hits a day times seven days a week that's twenty-eight. So that's $210 a week. But I will give it to you for $150,"

"Wow, that's a lot. But my grandma gives me $300 a week because she doesn't want me to work and go to school. My mom doesn't know she gives me so much. It's our little secret and I have so much in my savings account. But I guess I can do $150." Sandy took the bags and two glass tubes she was given.

"Just do it as I showed you, it's easy to do. I'll get back to you in a week. See ya later." Ruby walked out of the room and closed the door,

Sandy looked at the big bag holding all the smaller bags and glass tubes and put them in her top drawer under her underwear. She looked at the time and soon it would be time for her next class. She had an hour, and she decided to take another hit before class. It was her public speaking class, and she had to give a presentation. ten minutes before she had to leave, she took out one of the baggies and one of the glass pipes. She put the powder in and lit the pipe and inhaled the white vapor as hard as she was able to. Within seconds, it hit her hard, and she experienced the room spinning, and then she was on top of the world. No one would hurt her or look down on her. She was a queen. She left her room and hurried down the path to class and rushed into the room. She sat down and her eyes darted all over the place and her hands kept moving from her hair to her face to her body. She had trouble sitting still and jiggled her foot. Other students already in the room glanced over at her in curiosity, and several looked at each other and raised their eyebrows at each other. Sandy did not notice. She was in her own world. The teacher came in and started the class. One by one people got up and gave their speeches. Finally, it was Sandy's turn, and she walked up to the front with her notes. The drug gave her courage, and she wasn't nervous but her mind was going a mile a minute. She was going to speak on Abortion and why she was against it. She didn't know how well it will be received since most instructors and college age students were pro-choice. She faced the class and looked at her notes and it was like they were dancing on the page before her.

Abortion is the....um...taking off...I mean taking OF..human life......A human fetus's heart , um it's heart beat.......starts at eighteen to twenty one days. And it has....um..brains...I mean brain waves....at six weeks......It starts to....um.....movement.....um...I mean it starts to move at eight.....weeks and it has its entire body is...um done...um I mean formed by then......It can....um...suck...suck its thumb by ten weeks and ....looks..like...looks like a ....baby at this....um stage....It can do somersaults...um...by...um.....twelve weeks...It feels painful....um..pain...at..umm twenty weeks.....It can survive....in the ....um.... no... I mean ..survive out of the...um womb....at twenty-two weeks. Abortion...abortions are performed....even...electively at..this..um...um...stage. There's a clinic....in...um...New...Mexico...um...New Mexico that does....elective abortions...for any reason abortions....at ...umm...up to thirty=two weeks....This is um....very shocking...This is..um...all...is all...proof...that...abortion....is.....wrong....and should....not be ...um legal....Human Life....is at....I mean goes at at....no....I mean........begins at....conception........That's all..."

She walked back to her seat and there was silence in the classroom, and no one clapped until the teacher finally said something.

"Well, that was certainly interesting. Let's move on to the next person. Jason Barnes, can you come up and do your presentation, please?"

Everyone finished, and the teacher said they were allowed to go. Sandy walked past the teacher's desk and he called out to her.

"Sandy, may I talk to you?"

Sandy walked over to him, nervous, not knowing what he was going to say.

"Are you O. K? Your presentation was wild and showed you were unprepared. Were you just not prepared for this?'"

Sandy didn't know what to say. "I don't know. I had a lot to say. and tried to say it. I had so many things come to my mind and I couldn't say them fast enough. The words on my sheets were dancing before my eyes."

"Sandy, are you on something? You are acting like you are." He stroked his chin with his hand.

Sandy wanted to get away from this conversation. She had the idea that anything she said would make the situation worse. "No, I am just tired. I haven't been sleeping. I am so tired and wired up." *Possibly he will buy that, she thought.*

He just stared at her for a minute. "O. K, but if you are having a problem, I want you to know you can come to me and talk."

Sandy nodded vigorously and then turned and rushed out of the room. She ran down the paths to her dorm and when she got there, she hurried in and into her room. She got a packet and the pipe out of her stash and lit it up and inhaled. That powerful, warm, intense, uplifting, invigorating feeling filled her and her five senses exploded. Colors were brighter, smells were more intense, sounds rang louder in her ears, touches made her tingle, and the only body sense not enhanced was her sense of taste, as she had no desire for food. In fact, she had no appetite whatsoever.

****

Sandy heard terrifying news. There was a rape on campus last week. She had asked why it wasn't in the news and was told it was being handled by the college and the campus police. That didn't sit right with Sandy, *But what can I do? she thought.* She didn't dwell on it long because it was time for another hit on her pipe. She was at the point where she wasn't able to live without it. She was up to $250 a week now on it and she lost twelve pounds. Even though she had boundless energy, she had lost interest in school and her future career goals. All she cared about was getting her meth. She had stopped taking her psych medication because she thought she didn't need them anymore. The meth gave her grand ideas and feelings of self-importance and ironically she had voices telling her she did not need them. She was not sleeping much at night and spent many nights prowling the streets in the dark, which she was now not afraid of. Her grades had plummeted to where the EOP director told her she was on academic probation and if she failed one more course she was out of college. She still had not passed her remedial math course much to her shame. Tonight she came home ready to take another hit, and she got the idea that she would do two hits instead of one. *If one feels amazing, then two must feel over the moon, And maybe I should take some Adderall too and be over several moons, she thought.* So she took two Adderall, then paused, and then took six more. She waited thirty minutes until they started taking effect. Then she brought out her pipe and two baggies. she put them all in her pipe and inhaled and inhaled until it was all gone. The rush came immediately, and it was unlike anything she had ever experienced. She fell back against her pillow and was pinned to her bed. The world swirled around her and she was floating. But suddenly she had a sharp pain in the center of her chest. It was so sharp and painful, and she gasped and cried out.

"Ahhhhhhhh. It hurts. Someone help me!"

But she couldn't catch her breath to scream loud and it came out like a gasp. The pain shot down her arm and became so intense she knew it was her heart. It was beating wildly, and she was able to hear it in her head. She could not sit up or even roll over. She started to see black spots in her vision and things were growing dark.

Suddenly, there was an explosion of pain and bright lights.......and then there was nothing.

They didn't find out she was dead for three days. The sad thing was that no one really missed her to know she was missing. It was the smell from her room that alerted them to her body. Her roommate just thought she was sleeping. They did an investigation, and the finding was that she died from a massive overdose of amphetamines that strained her heart until it stopped.

Jesus turned to Rebecca and smiled at her. "Do you see what you did in that one person's life and the ripple down effect it had on thousands, even millions of others? You saved a life from drugs and death. You enabled her to finish college and go on to have a career where she helped hundreds of others. She formed a group that changed the way colleges handle rape and assault cases across the country and literally saved thousands of people from being raped and assaulted by making colleges increase their security on campus. All because you touched one solitary life.

Then He showed her another scene from her life. Rebecca was so touched by the last one that she anxiously waited to see what He was going to show her next

CHAPTER SIX

Katie was running late and was going to miss the bus. She had overslept again, and she woke up once again nauseous and sick to her stomach. She missed the bus yesterday and her mother threw a fit when she had to drive her to school and if she had to do it two days in a row, there would be hell to pay. Katie wasn't really in the mood for that. She was too queasy to eat anything, so she grabbed her books, ran out the door, and headed down the street to the bus stop. Lisa and Jane were already at the bus stop waiting and they waved when they watched her huffing and puffing down the street. She stopped in front of them, trying to catch her breath.

"Hi.....guys....I.....made....it....today.....I..was...afraid...I..was.....gonna ....miss it."

Lisa laughed. "You need to get it together Katie, you're a wreck and you didn't even put make-up on."

Katie smiled. "I.....barely..had..time....to..get..dressed. I've....been...so...tired lately." She took a deep breath and let it out slowly. "And...my boobs ache...like....crazy."

Lisa looked at Jane and raised her eyebrows, then she looked back at Katie. "When was your last period?"

Just then, the bus came and Katie didn't get to answer that question, they bounded up the steps on the bus and took their usual seats and Lisa repeated her question to Katie.

"Um, I don't know because I'm irregular. I get one every other month and sometimes skip two months but you're not asking why I think you're asking, are you?" She gave her a mirthless smile.

Lisa raised her eyebrows. "Of course I am. You've done it with Derek, right?"

Katie turned bright red. "Um, yeah."

Lisa crossed her arms across her chest. "Well, it stands to reason, then it's possible you could be pregnant, Katie."

Katie put her hand over her mouth. "That would be the worst thing possible and my mother would kick me out of the house. I don't know what Derek would do. He has a lousy part-time job, and he's a senior in high school just like me, we could never support ourselves. Unless we drop out of school and that's unthinkable, I mean we're seniors and we only have seven more months until graduation."

Jane touched Katie's arm. "You could always abort and that would solve the problem easily."

Katie put her other hand over her mouth. "How could I do that? It's a baby!"

"No, it's not, it's just tissue at this stage so it's no big deal," Jane said.

"I heard the heart starts beating at 21 days," Lisa said.

Jane tossed her hair over her shoulder. "It doesn't matter. It has no working brain at this point so it knows and feels nothing, so as I said, it's really no big deal."

"Well, before you worry over this, get a pregnancy test. Find out for sure." Lisa said.

"I'll do it after school. I'll take the 105 bus and get off the bus at Randall Street where Wal Mart is and then walk home. It's not that far."

Katie spent the rest of the day worrying over whether or not she was pregnant and did not concentrate very hard. When the final bell rang, she raced out to the bus and got on. She watched for the stop she wanted and got off and headed for the store. She looked for the aisle where the tests would be and found them. There were over a dozen of them and she couldn't figure out which one to get so she looked at each one and decided on the one that said "yes" or "no" instead of just having a blue line. That way, there would be no doubt. She felt self-conscious bringing it up to the register, and she was terrified someone she recognized would witness her buying it. She lived in a small community where people recognized each other and it was easy to run into someone that you knew and Katie had done that many times before. She handed the box to the cashier who looked at the box and then looked at her for a moment before she rang it up and asked her for the money. Katie paid for it and stuffed it in her backpack, and then left the store for home. It was a twenty-minute walk home, and it gave Katie plenty of time to think., and think she did. She couldn't think of what she would do if the test came up positive, all she understood is if she kept the baby her mom would definitely kick her out of the house. There was no doubt of that in her mind because her mom had told her that several times before with such preciseness, it left no doubts in her mind. But could she kill her baby and then live with that knowledge, or was it not a baby like Jane said? *I must do more research if this is positive, she thought.* She finally arrived home and her mom's car was not there. Katie smiled with relief. She brought her bag into her room and then hurried into the bathroom and opened up the box. She grabbed the stick and sat down and peed on it and then set it down on the counter. She looked at her watch and timed it for three minutes. Those minutes ticked by slowly, and finally, the time was up so she grabbed the stick and held it, willing herself to glance at it. Finally, she turned it around and her heart sank, it said YES. There was no doubt or ambiguity in reading the results of the test, it was there in plain English, in three simple letters that spelled out the word. In no uncertain terms, she was pregnant. She, Katie Marie Stanford, age 18, was pregnant, and she looked in the mirror and ran her hand through her brown hair with golden highlights that flowed down to the middle of her back. She looked at her flawless honey complexion and cute upturned nose and rosebud lips. She stared into her chocolate brown, gold-flecked eyes with long, thick eyelashes under perfectly stenciled eyebrows that lived on a heart-shaped face. She knew she was pretty, and she was popular but those things were not going to help her now or get her out of this situation. She couldn't think what would so she turned off her phone and didn't answer it or go on social media the whole day or night.

****

The next day, she arrived at the bus stop early. When the other girls arrived, they took one glance at Katie and figured out the answer.

"Why didn't you answer your phone? It's positive, isn't it? I can tell by your face. I'm so sorry Katie." Jane came over and gave her a hug.

As soon as they parted, Lisa grabbed Katie. "Oh Katie, I don't know what to say.' Then she pulled away. "What are you gonna do?"

Katie had tears in her eyes. "I have no idea. I'm telling Derek today and I will find out what he has to say and I will need to make a decision soon. I don't even know how far along I am since I have no clue when my last period was or even when I could have gotten pregnant."

Then the bus came, and they all got on. When they got to school, Katie looked for Derek and found him by the front door.

"Derek, we need to talk."

"Hey, Katie." He pulled her into a hug and kissed her. "What's up?"

"I will be blunt. I'm pregnant." She put her hands in front of her and clasped them together.

"Whoa, I thought we used condoms." He held a hand out to her.

"Um, yeah, remember they broke three times?" She put a hand on her hip.

He looked at her sheepishly. "Yeah, I guess I remember that. What are you going to do about it?"

"What do you mean I am going to do about it? It's half yours too." She put her other hand on her hip.

"I mean, we can't keep it. We are seven months away from graduating from high school. I only work a part-time job. You want to go to college and I want to go to a trade school. It's not fair to us or the kid to have it now."

She nodded her head. "Yeah, that makes sense. But I don't have any money."

"Don't worry about that. I will come up with it. My Dad would give me the money because he would not want me to have a kid right now and knows we ain't ready for one. So make the appointment and I'll take care of the money. I will go with you to the appointment, too."

She gave him and hug and a kiss. "Thanks for being great about this. I love you!"

Then the bell rang, and they walked into the building and into their classrooms.

****

Katie dialed the number to the clinic.

"Hello, Dawson Women's Clinic."

"Um, hi, I need to make an appointment for an abortion."

"Sure. How far along are you and when was your last period/"

"I don't know. I'm irregular."

"That's O.K. We can do a sonogram. But our prices go by how far along you are. Prices start at $350 for 4-5 weeks $400 for 6-7 weeks $450 7-8 weeks, $500 got 8-9 weeks, $550- for 10-12 weeks, $650 for 13-14 weeks, $750 for 15-16 weeks, $850 for 17-18 weeks, $950 for 19-20 weeks and $1200 for 20-24 weeks. You probably should bring in at least $650 and if you're less, you take the rest home. We can have you come in 4 days on the 24th at 8:00 in the morning. What's your name?"

"That's fine. My name is Katie Stanford."

"O. K Katie, we will see you then."

Katie called Derek and told him what they said. He told her he would get the $650 and he would pick her up at 7:30 that morning.

Katie wasn't a hundred percent sure about this. She wanted to go online and look up pictures of unborn babies and aborted babies but she was afraid it would sway her mind against it. She needed to be firm about this, but, she still was sad because deep in her heart she understood it was a baby, her baby. She took a walk to the park and sat on the swings and rocked back and forth and a tear escaped her eye and rolled down her cheek. She didn't bother to wipe it away, and she didn't see the lady approach her, being so lost in her thoughts. The lady sat down in the swing next to her.

"Hey sweetie, are you O. K?"

Katie jumped, shocked to have someone sitting next to her. "Oh, what? Um.....yeah...I guess I am."

The lady smiled sadly at her. "You don't seem O.K. I noticed tears on your cheek."

Katie touched her cheek. "Yeah, I guess I am."

The lady held out her hand. "My name is Rebecca. What's yours?"

Katie shook her hand. "Mine's Katie."

"Hi, Katie. I realize you don't know me but I'm a good listener." And Rebecca cocked her head to one side.

Katie looked down at her lap and fidgeted with her hands. "I'm 18 and a high school senior and I'm pregnant."

Rebecca nodded her head. "Wow, yeah, that must be really heavy on you and I'm sure it was not planned."

Katie shook her head. "No, it's most certainly not. I graduate in seven months and I'm supposed to go to college. Same with my boyfriend and we talked it over and we're terminating the pregnancy. I have an appointment in four days and we feel that's the best thing for us and for the baby."

Rebecca was silent for a moment. "But you are having tears over it so your heart must not be totally into it."

Katie looked up at the sky. "Yeah, I'm not sure if it's a baby I am killing and if it is if it's right. My friend says the heart starts beating at 21 days and it looks like a baby by eight weeks, and by twelve weeks it can suck its thumb."

"Yes, those things are true. It is a baby, right from conception it is a unique new life with its own set of DNA that will never be repeated, and the baby develops very quickly. Some will deny it, but some will say they can even feel pain as early as eight weeks. How far along are you?"

Katie looked at her. "I'm not sure. I am irregular and don't know when I could've conceived."

Rebecca reached out and touched her arm. "I know a place that does free sonograms and you could find out and you could see what your baby looks like right now. They have an amazing 3D sonogram and we could go right now."

Katie raised her eyebrows. "Really? I think I'd like that."

"O.K. Why don't we go? It's only five minutes from here." Rebecca said.

Katie stood up and followed Rebecca to her car and got in and they drove to the crisis pregnancy center the next town over. They pulled up to a tan building with a brown roof with a sign outside that said Life Choices

Center. They got out and Katie followed Rebecca into the building, they went up to the receptionist and Rebecca told them she was there with someone for a sonogram. They told her it would be a few minutes, and they sat down. Katie looked around the room. It was painted pale pink with light tan carpeting and there were pictures of mothers and babies on the walls and pictures of babies in different stages of fetal development. There were potted plants on the floor that was four feet high and plants on the window sills. Soon they were called in and taken to a small room, there was a table in the middle of the room and the lady had Katie get up on it. She lowered her pants, and the lady squirted some cool jelly onto her stomach. Then she put a probe onto the area and she moved it around and then the baby jumped onto the screen. Right away, they could recognize the baby moving around and was quite active. The lady took some measurements.

"You are just about twelve weeks pregnant. Here is your baby. Your little one is perfectly formed, just notice her arms, legs toes, and fingers and here's her head and her eyes nose, and mouth and look, she is sucking her thumb! I love when they do that! She is about three inches long from her head to her bottom not counting her legs. Here are some pictures to take home with you."

Katie watched the screen, mesmerized by her baby. She could clearly recognize that it was a little baby in there, bouncing and jumping around, but she still wondered how she could give birth to this baby and was it fair to bring her into the world when they weren't ready to be parents. Not to mention how it would ruin their lives. Rebecca could see the conflicted expression on Katie's face. They finished up and left the room. The lady took them into another room with a desk in the middle and there were more potted plants on the floor. The walls were painted a soft yellow and had more pictures of babies and unborn babies. Rebecca and Katie sat down in the two chairs that were in front of the desk.

"Hello, my name is Sandra. I'm a counselor here at Life Choices. How are you doing today?"

Katie smiled a shy smile. "I'm not doing so well I guess."

Sandra cocked her head to one side. "Is this a wanted pregnancy or are you considering abortion?"

Katie looked down at her hands. "I have an abortion scheduled in four days."

"Oh, O. K. How do you feel now that you've seen your baby on the sonogram?" Sandra leaned forward in her chair.

Katie looked up and rubbed the back of her neck. "I'm conflicted now. I understand now it's a baby but it would be awful to the baby and to me and my boyfriend if I had it now."

"How would it be awful to the baby?" Sandra folded her hands on the desk.

"I would be kicked out of my home and I'm supposed to graduate in seven months and so is my boyfriend. Where would we live? How would we support ourselves? We wouldn't be able to go to college. Our whole futures would be ruined and the baby would be raised in poverty." Katie felt more confident with each word that she said.

Sandra nodded her head. "Yes, those things may be true. Have you thought about adoption? There are thousands of men and women who would love to adopt your baby and would love it and cherish it and give it the best home possible."

Katie furrowed her eyebrows. She hadn't thought about that option and it intrigued her. "I never thought of that. That actually sounds like an interesting idea and we wouldn't have our lives ruined and the baby wouldn't have to die."

Rebecca spoke up. "I think that is the ideal option, Katie. The best idea for both you and your baby."

Katie nodded. "How do I find out more about that? I need to talk to my boyfriend but I doubt he would object to this."

"Right next door to here is an adoption agency. I will call over and find out if they can have you come over today."

She picked up the phone and made the call. She was on for a few minutes and then hung up.

"They would love to have you come right now. Why don't you go over and talk to them?"

So, Rebecca and Katie walked next door to Loving Arms Adoption Agency and walked right up to the receptionist. She called back and almost immediately a tall, stately looking woman came out. She had to be six feet tall and as thin as a reed and she had short brown highlighted hair brushed back in waves. Her lips had a dark pink lipstick and were thick and full and above that was a strong, long nose and eyes the color of arctic blue ice. She came over to them and shook their hands and they all introduced themselves.

Rebecca spoke first. "Hi, this is Katie who's considering adoption and I'm Rebecca, a friend."

"My name is Rose Diamond. I am the director here, please come into my office."

They walked into an office that had dark mahogany wood furniture. There was a huge L-shaped desk and a bookshelf that was full of books. There were plants on the bookshelf and on the desk and a big four-foot potted plant on the floor in the corner. They sat down in two chairs that had deep cushions on them.

"So, Katie, you're considering placing your baby with a Christian family? That is a selfless, wonderful, saintly, thing to do. It is also the most unselfish thing you can do. You will give your baby a wonderful life and you will be able to pursue your own dreams. It's a win-win situation for you and your baby. How far along are you?"

Katie smiled at her words. They made her feel so good inside. "I am 12 weeks."

"So, you're going to be entering into your second trimester. We would need to find you a doctor for prenatal care. Would you like to browse through a book that has couples that are looking to adopt?"

That excited Katie. "Yes, I would."

Rose got up and walked to her bookcase and pulled out what looked like a large photo album and handed it to Katie. Katie opened it up and there was a smiling, beautifully dressed, handsome couple on the page. She read the paragraph that described them. They were in their early thirties and couldn't give birth to children of their own. They had one adopted child, a three-year-old boy, and the husband was a computer programmer and his wife stayed home to care for their son. They lived in a large home with a swimming pool. They seemed lovely to Katie. And then she turned the page. There was another couple standing there, smiling. They were in their late twenties and also had an adopted child, a two-year-old little girl. The husband was the vice president of a company and his wife stayed home with their daughter. They lived in a huge home that also had a swimming pool and they seemed like dream parents to Katie. Page after page, she witnessed wonderful people who would make great parents.

"How do I choose? They all seem so wonderful?"

Rose laughed. "I know, right? Isn't that beautiful? Does one stand out to you?"

Katie furrowed her eyebrows and twisted her lips. "Hmmm, well, this one I guess. She opened it back up and found the right page. It was a couple in their thirties with an adopted three-year-old daughter. The husband was president of his own company. They had a six-bedroom home with an indoor swimming pool and ten acres of land with a huge lake and a stable with horses. They owned a large boat and went sailing in the ocean and the three of them took trips around the world. They showed the little girl's room, and it looked decorated like a fantasy land. The mother stayed home with the little girl and didn't work. Katie couldn't imagine a more perfect home. SHE wanted to live there. She couldn't believe all that transpired since meeting that kind lady. When she woke up this morning, she was filled with despair, but now, she had a spark of hope, a feeling that things might just be O.K and she won't have to live with the pain of knowing she killed her child.

Rose took the book and looked at the page. "Oh my, yes. They ARE a great choice, I must say so myself. Your child will be well taken care of with this family. The little one will have everything they want and need and could possibly ask for. Now the questions that remain. What are YOUR needs? The family will pay for all your pregnancy expenses, including medical, your maternity clothes, and give you a subsidy to live on to help you out. If you do not have a place to live, they will provide that too until the baby is born and for a time after that. You can also do an open adoption and still be in the baby's life after she is born."

Katie listen with wide eyes. She was amazed that every problem and need would be taken care of. She would give birth to the baby, finish high school and go to college in the fall. Nothing would change. Except, of course, she would be going through a pregnancy and delivery of a baby. She would need to find out if her mother would let her live in the home while she was pregnant. If not, Rose said the people would pay for a place for her to live. The baby would be due two months before graduation.

Katie nodded her head. 'I want to do this. It is perfect. I won't need to abort and can finish high school and I can go to college in the fall. I don't know if my mom will kick me out, that is something I will need to find out. I must also talk to my boyfriend. I can do that tonight. Can I talk to you tomorrow?"

Rose smiled. "There's no rush. We will do this on your time. Talk to your parents and your boyfriend and find out what your needs are going to be and then get back to me and we will make an adoption plan."

They left and Rebecca drove her home. She made sure to give Katie her phone number, and they agreed they would talk as soon as Katie told her mother and her boyfriend.

Katie walked into her house and her mother was in the kitchen. She walked over and stood outside the doorway for a while. Finally, she thought, it was now or never. She walked in and stood by the counter. Her mom was at the sink doing dishes.

"Mom, I need to talk to you about something important."

Her mom glanced over at her briefly and went back to doing the dishes. "Yes, what is it, Katie?"

"I don't know how to say it. It's going to make you mad and disappointed in me. But I have a plan that's going to make it all work out all right. The plan will make it fine in the end and nothing will change for my future."

Her mom shut off the water and turned to face her."What are you trying to say?"

"I'm pregnant, mom. But I'm giving the baby up for adoption. I can still graduate and still go to college in the fall."

Her mom just stared at her for a long while. She slowly shook her head. "I can't believe you did this, Katie. What were you thinking? What were you thinking about having sex? This is why you wait until marriage to engage in sex and not before. I don't know what to do with you. My first instinct is to kick you out. I always said that's what I would do if you ever came to me like this. Are you serious about adoption?"

Katie vigorously nodded her head. "Yes, mom. I even found the family I would like to give the baby to. They are wonderful. They have lots of money and live in a mansion and own a huge boat and go on vacations around the world. They have a three-year-old adopted little girl who has this magical bedroom and there's an indoor swimming pool and a huge lake and horses. And I can do an open adoption and still be in the baby's life after she is born, and you'd be able to as well! And I viewed the baby, mom. It was a 3D ultrasound. It's little baby with a complete body and she was sucking her thumb, look, here's a picture."

Katie's mom softened her expression. She smiled a soft smile. "That sounds like a wonderful and amazing family, Katie and you are handling this mistake responsibly. But, out of curiosity. How did you find this place to get the ultrasound and find the family?"

"I was sitting on the swings at the park crying and a lady came up to me. She was so kind so I told her what was going on. I told her I scheduled an abortion but didn't feel that great about it. She took me to a pregnancy center. They also told me they will pay all expenses and will give me a stipend for living expenses while pregnant. For clothes and anything else I may need."

Her mother nodded. "I would like to go with you when you go back. I would like to meet the parents too and be involved in this whole thing. I'm glad we will be able to play a small part in the baby's life after it's born. I'm actually proud of you, Katie, for how you are handling this. Yes, you made a mistake, but you are making good choices to fix the mistake." Then she took Katie in her arms and held her close.

Katie had tears in her eyes while she was in her mom's arms. She had expected anger and shouting and being told to pack her bags. This was so unexpected but so good. She relished in the love her mother was giving her. Then they parted.

"I need to talk to Derek and tell him the plans will be changed. I have no clue what he will say. But he doesn't want a baby so I doubt he will fight the adoption. I'm gonna call him now."

She walked into her room and flopped down on her bed. She dialed Derek's number.

"Hello?"

"Hey Derek, It's me. I have some news for you. I'm not having an abortion. I'm going to..."

He interrupted her. "WHAT? I thought we decided it was for the best for us and for the baby. How can you go and change your mind now? I don't want a baby messing everything up!"

"DEREK! Will you let me finish what I was saying, please? We are not going to have a baby to raise and care for. Plus abortion isn't exactly best for the baby, when you think about it, just saying. But I spoke to an adoption agency, and I picked out a family They have an adopted little girl and a mansion, an indoor swimming pool, horses, a lake, a boat, and more. They are gonna pay for all expenses. And we can visit the baby after it's born and play a small part in its life since it will be an open adoption. It's perfect."

There was silence on the other end of the phone. She almost thought he hung up. "Um, O.K. I guess. That kinda does sound neat. The baby would receive all that. We wouldn't be able to give it all that. And yeah, I guess abortion isn't exactly best for the baby when you think about it. I'm all for this."

Katie breathed a sigh of relief. "Thank you, Derek, I'm so glad. I promise you it will all work out." Then they hung up the phone.

Then Katie decided to call Rebecca and tell her the news. She dialed her number.

"Hello?"

"Hi Rebecca, It's me, Katie. I wanted to tell you my mom is all for this and she actually said she was proud of me. And my boyfriend said he is for it too. So it is all set. I am going for the open adoption."

"Oh Katie, I'm so happy for you. This is such a great choice and you will be blessed by it. It will all work out in the end, you'll see. I will be by you every step of the way. I consider you my new friend now."

Katie felt such warmth flow through the phone. "I consider you my new friend too, Rebecca. Thank you for everything!"

Katie hung up the phone and laid back on her bed and looked up at the ceiling. She had a smile on her face and she rubbed the small mound growing on her lower stomach. She realized it was going to be alright, and she knew she could go to sleep tonight with no worries.

CHAPTER SEVEN

K atie woke up feeling excited. Today she was going to meet the parents of her baby. She jumped in the shower and then got dressed. She chose a pretty pink dress with small flowers on it and her pink sandals. She styled her hair and put on makeup. She wanted to look her best. She hurried down the stairs and into the kitchen where her mother was making breakfast. She wasn't starving, but she knew she needed to eat for the baby. Her mother had made bacon and eggs and placed a plate in front of her. She managed to get it all down but her queasiness was bothering her. She took some deep breaths, trying to keep the food down. Soon it was 9:30, and they were meeting at 10:00 so Katie and her mom grabbed their pocketbooks and headed out to the car. Katie's mom asked if she could meet the parent's and Katie wholeheartedly agreed. It only took fifteen minutes to get to the adoption agency and Katie's mom parked the car. They walked into the building and up to the receptionist to tell her they were there. Not even five minutes later Rose Diamond came out and brought them back to her office. When they walked in, there was a handsome couple and a small girl already sitting there. The woman had long, platinum blonde hair that hung down her back in spiral curls. Her eyes were a striking aqua blue and her nose was small and upturned. She had a perfect creamy white complexion with no marks or blemishes. She was dressed in designer clothing and had a Coach pocketbook. The man had golden tan skin and dirty blonde hair that was cut short on the sides and longer on top. He, too, had blue eyes, and a finely chiseled nose. He was dressed in black cargo pants and a white button-down shirt. The little girl had golden blonde hair that hung down her back in ringlets and she had light blue colored eyes. She was wearing a blue, red, and white Tommy Hilfiger dress with red socks and white sandals. She smiled at Katie when she walked into the room. Both of them stood when Katie, her mom, and Derek came into the room and held out their hands.

"Hello, my name is Kristen. So glad to meet you, Katie!"

"Hey there, my name is Byron. I'm also glad to meet you, Katie."

Katie, Derek, and her mom shook their hands and then sat down.

Rose smiled at everyone that was there. "I am so excited for this meeting and that I could bring you all together. I've got a good feeling about this!"

Kristen looked at Katie. "Would you like to ask us some questions?"

Katie nodded. "What's your home like? I saw some pictures, and it looked beautiful."

Kristen smiled broadly. "Yes, we live in a 10,000 square foot home and it has seven bedrooms and eight bathrooms. There is a huge eat-in kitchen and a dining room. There's a large living room with a fireplace and a huge family room where Julie has her toys. There is an indoor pool off the family room and a fitness center next to that. Julie's room is set up like a magic princess castle and has a canopy bed and a playhouse built-in. Outside we've got tennis courts, gardens and a large lake we go water skiing and jet skiing on. We've got a barn with eight horses and Julie has her own pony. There is a large playground and a large playhouse that is two stories tall and has electricity in it and realistic kitchen appliances and living room furniture. There is a bedroom on top with a bed. We also own a 150-foot yacht that we go sailing on almost every weekend."

Katie listened with wide eyes. "How do you discipline your child?"

Kristen nodded. "We NEVER use physical discipline and use time-outs and restricting privileges. But we use discipline sparingly and try to use positive reinforcements."

"Do you have any other family?"

"Oh yes, I have my parents who live on our property in a 3 bedroom home. I have two sisters and a brother and many nieces and nephews. Byron's parents live a half-hour away and he has a brother and a sister and nieces and nephews."

"Do you have a nanny?"

Kristen looked hesitant. "Well, yes, but she only helps out. I do most of the care and believe in being hands-on with Julie."

"Do you have any pets?"

"Oh yes, we've got two golden retrievers, three cats, four birds, two hamsters, rabbits, and a hedgehog. Julie adores animals."

Katie laughed. "That sounds awesome!"

Katie didn't know what else to ask. Rose jumped in. "This will be an open adoption."

Byron nodded. "Yes, we would want you all to be a part of the baby's life. Almost like godparents."

Katie rubbed her hands together. "That is wonderful and just what I want."

Derek and Katie's mom nodded.

"You will get a $2500 a month stipend until the baby is six months old. Your medical bills will be paid for and any other pregnancy-related expenses. Kristen would like to be in the delivery room. Are you O.K. with that, Katie?" Rose asked.

"Oh yes, I want that very much. I want her to be first to hold the baby." Katie said.

"I was able to induce lactation and breastfeed Julie. She still nurses a few times a day. I would like to nurse the baby in the delivery room if that's O.K." Kristen asked

Katie was wide-eyed. "You can breastfeed an adopted baby? Wow, I never knew that! I'm impressed! That is fine with me! How old is Julie?"

"Julie is three years old. I believe in toddler and extended breastfeeding. They still get the benefits after they turn one and the benefits continue for as long as you nurse the child. I believe in attachment parenting. I use a baby sling and hold the baby most of the day. Byron and the nanny help some. I do not believe in letting babies and children cry it out. We eat very healthily with limited sugar.'

Katie had tears in her eyes. "I can't believe all this. I don't think I could find better parents for my baby. I want you to adopt my baby!"

Kristen and Byron started crying. Kristen grabbed Katie's hands. "Oh thank you, Katie. You won't be sorry!"

Rose brought out papers to sign. "We will sign an adoption plan and the adoption will be finalized when the baby is six months old." Everyone signed the papers.

Katie looked at Kristen. "Would you like some sonogram pictures of the baby?"

Kristen nodded with tears in her eyes.

Katie handed her the pictures and Kristen and Byron cried over them.

Then everyone left for home.

****

Katie invited Kristen and Byron to her twenty-week sonogram. They would find out the sex of the baby. They met at the doctor's office and walked in. They were led to a small room with a table and a sonogram machine. It was a 3D machine that showed the baby perfectly.

The sonogram technician rolled the transceiver over Katie's baby bump. "The baby looks healthy and normal. Do you want to find out what it is?"

Everyone nodded.

"Well, congratulations, you are having a boy!"

Kristin was beside herself and started crying. "I'll have a girl and a boy! How perfect is that?"

Byron also had tears in his eyes. "A son. I always wanted a son! A daughter and a son, how amazing!"

The technician printed out some pictures and Katie gave them to Kristen. Then they all left the building and left for home.

Kristen followed Katie to every doctor's appointment and invited her to their home for a meal and to swim in the pool. Katie was treated like family, and so were her mother and Derek. The pregnancy proceeded normally and soon it was time for Katie to have the baby. They all met at the hospital and Katie was put into a gown and hooked up to a fetal monitor. Kristen and her mother held her hand through the contractions and Katie did a marvelous job. The baby boy was born at 2:00 in the afternoon and he weighed six pounds, twelve ounces, and was twenty inches long. He had a full head of blonde hair and beautiful long blonde eyelashes. Kristen got to nurse him in the delivery room. Byron and Derek joined them and the nurse took a picture of all of them.

Soon it was time for Katie to say goodbye to the baby but she knew she would see him again. She kissed his little head and handed him to Byron who put him in a car seat. They left for home. Katie had some sad tears but understood she did the right thing for her baby. She was giving him the best life possible.

****

Katie saw her son, Brandon, throughout the years and got to watch him grow up. He was a smart boy and did well in his private prep school and took an interest in science. He graduated high school as valedictorian and went to an ivy league college. He became a scientist and got his Ph.D. in chemistry. He wanted to find a cure for cancer, or at least a viable treatment. His father funded him to open his own lab and hire the necessary people. Brandon had gone on to find an amazing treatment for a form of cancer and was hailed a miracle worker. Katie was so proud of him. One day she sat down and talked to him.

"Brandon, I am so proud of the man you have become. You have saved countless lives. I almost aborted you and realize how big a hole that would have left in so many people's lives. I hope you understand why I gave you up for adoption."

"Yes, Mama Katie, I do understand and I am so grateful for the opportunities you gave me by making that unselfish choice. I have had an amazing life and my future seems just as bright. Thank you for making the adoption decision and giving me life." He reached over and hugged her tightly.

Katie hugged him back and knew she had made the right decision. Her son was living proof of that. She smiled and laid her head on his shoulder, and knew the future would only get brighter.

Rebecca had tears in her eyes when she realized she had a hand in making this all happen. By helping Katie, thousands, if not millions of lives were saved by Brandon's discoveries. And she saved Brandon himself. All because she intervened in one solitary life.

CHAPTER EIGHT

There was a distant noise in the background, a buzzing noise and it grew louder and louder until it jarred Katie awake and she realized it was her alarm clock urging her to wake up. She reached over and slammed her hand onto the button that shut it off and missed, knocking the clock off onto the floor. Groaning, she turned over in bed and leaned down, and reached for the clock, which was just out of arms reach. She stretched her arm and moved her body down a few inches and then — BAM.....She found herself on the floor head first with the alarm clock in her hand. *REALLY, she thought. Is this a sign of how my day is going to be?* She untangled her legs from the blankets and got up from the floor and groaned. Her muscles ached, so she stretched out her arms and twisted her body and she bent her neck to the side by pressing on her chin — crack.. crack.. crack... — her neck cracked in a staccato rhythm that released the pressure and tension in her neck and head. She walked to the closet and picked out an outfit for the day. She chose a pair of black Calvin Klein skinny jeans and a white and pink Hollister brand t-shirt and grabbed her pink Sketcher sneakers and got dressed. She reached for her liquid foundation to put on her face and her hand hit it and it fell to the floor, splattering all over. *DAMN! What a morning, I hope it doesn't get worse, she thought.* She bent over and cleaned the mess up and lamented the loss of a $12 bottle of makeup. She finished her makeup and her hair and walked out to the kitchen. Her stomach had not been acting right for a while now, especially in the morning so she skipped eating breakfast. She grabbed a 12-ounce container of orange juice and headed out the door to the bus stop. She tentatively took some sips of the juice and her nausea abated a little. When she got to the bus stop, Lisa and Jane were there waiting.

"Hey Katie, how are ya? How are ya feeling?" Lisa asked

"Yeah, hi Katie. Are you STILL feeling sick to your stomach?" Jane asked as she walked over to Katie and gave her a hug.

Katie moaned and wanted to sit down. "Yeah, it's been weeks now. It comes, and it goes and it's worse in the morning and when I go to bed. My boobs also are huge and hurt like hell."

Jane looked at Lisa and raised her eyebrows. "Katie, seriously, why haven't you thought of pregnancy?"

Katie looked horrified, her mouth open and her eyes wide. "I really can't be. I really can't. That would be the worse thing in the whole wide world and my life would be over!"

Jane put her hand on Katie's shoulder. "When was your last period?"

"I don't have any idea. I don't keep track plus I am so irregular. It's been a few months is all I can say right now."

Jane squeezed Katie's shoulder. "It's not the end of the world. There's the option of abortion and it's a totally legit option. It's a simple medical procedure and you go back to your life with no more worries or a baby."

"I heard the baby's heart starts beating at 21 days and the brain waves can be detected by 6 weeks. And it starts looking like a baby at 8 weeks and can suck its thumb and do somersaults by 10 weeks." Lisa said.

"Oh please. The brain is the size of a grain of sand or a piece of rice. It has no idea of what's happening to it and has no self-awareness. It experiences no pain, and it's only tissue in the shape of a baby. And it doesn't even look like a real baby until the third trimester. Only a red alien-looking thing before that." Jane said and threw her hair over her shoulder.

Katie stared at her two friends and couldn't think of what to say. They both had legitimate points to make, and she didn't know who was more right. *I must research this more, she thought.* The bus came, and they all got on. It was agonizing for Katie because the driving made her nausea worse. Finally, they got to school and got off the bus and they walked and found their cliques. Katie walked with Jane and Lisa over to where the cool and popular girls hung out. There was a lot of talk about clothes, shoes, and boys but nothing substantial, and Katie had too much on her mind to contribute to the nonsense. The bell rang, and they all hurried into the building and into their homerooms. Katie could not concentrate the whole day and all she wanted to do was go to a store and buy a pregnancy test. She decided she would take the 105 bus and get off a block from Wal-Mart and walk the 1/4 mile home. And that is what she did when the dismissal bell rang at 2:45. She got on the 105 number bus and rode it to the block before Wal mart and got off. It was a quick walk to get to the store. She searched the store and found where the tests were and were astonished at how many she had to choose from. She chose one that was easy to read and would tell her a simple yes or no instead of the ambiguous blue or pink line. She hurried to the register, self-conscious of the other shoppers. This was a small community and everyone seemed to recognize everyone and the chances of her being spotted with this test were high. But she made it to the register and while the cashier gave her the hairy eyeball, no one else saw what she bought. She paid for it and made the long trek home. When she got home, no one else was home, and she was so glad. She walked into the bathroom and opened the box, and pulled out the stick. She sat on the toilet and peed on the stick and sat it on the counter. The three minutes she had to wait were the longest three minutes of her life. Finally, she grabbed the stick and looked. Chills spread up her spine as waves of nausea coursed through her body, while her hands trembled as she held the stick that spelled out YES as clear as day. And she was told there were no false positives with these tests. Either you had the pregnancy hormone in your body or you did not and Katie had the pregnancy hormone in her body. She sat there for a while in stunned silence and was as still as a statue. The only thing on her body moving was a tear that ran down her cheek and landed on her shirt. Finally, she got up and took the test and box, and wandered into her room. She carefully wrapped the box up with other garbage and put it in her garbage can. She decided to go for a walk. She wandered to the park down the road and sat on the swings. She swung back and forth as the tears ran down her face. The cool air blew across her face and she thought about the holidays coming up. Her family would be getting together and she wondered how they would all treat her if they found out. Her mother had said she would kick her out of the house if she had a baby. Where would she go? How would she graduate and raise a baby? She would need to drop out of school months from her graduation. College would be out of the question. How would she support a baby? What would Derek say? He wouldn't want to be a father now. He had plans to go to a trade school. He would need to give all that up and work full-time at some minimum wage job, and so would she. They would struggle for the rest of their lives and so would their children. Was it fair to bring this baby into the world? She knew deep in her heart that it was a baby but she would need to harden her heart if she wanted to end the pregnancy and end her child's life. She decided to call Derek. It would be better to call him than do this in person.

"Hello?"

"Um, Derek.....It's Katie."

"Hey, Katie. How are ya? I was gonna call you later."

Katie dug her toe into the rocks below her. "I've got something to tell you. It's hard to say but I'm pregnant. I took the test, and it came back as yes, as clear as day and there is no doubt."

There was silence on the phone and she thought he had hung up. "This is awful. The end of the world. The end of all our plans and dreams. We can't have this baby, Katie. Think of your own goals and dreams. How will you do them with a baby? How will I support a baby on minimum wage?"

Katie sighed a huge sigh. "Yeah, you're probably right. I thought about all those things. It's just so hard because I understand it's a baby."

Katie heard him breathing heavily. "Yeah, Katie, I know it is too. But think of the terrible life it will have living in poverty. It will never acquire all the things it wants and life will always be a struggle. It's not fair to us and it's not fair to the baby. It's the kindest thing we can do right now for the baby, honestly."

Katie's tears flowed down her cheeks and her shoulder heaved up and down. "I know. I know. I will make an appointment tomorrow. I'm flat out of money of course. "

"That's not a problem. I can get it from my dad. He wouldn't want me to have a baby so I'm sure he will help. Let me know how much to ask from him."

"O.K I will. I will talk to you tomorrow."

They hung up and Kaite walked home. She walked past the living room and her mom called out hello. She decided to go in and tell her mother the plans."

"Mom, I've bad news but I am taking care of it. I'm pregnant and I am calling a clinic tomorrow to get an appointment to take care of it. I just wanted to let you know in case I suffer complications." She said it as fast as she could.

Her mom stood up and walked over to her and put her arms around her. "I'm sorry this happened to you and I'm glad you are taking care of it so it doesn't ruin your life. You can give birth to babies when you are done with college, acquire a good job, and are married to someone with a good job. I don't want to see you or a child struggle and suffer. Do you need a ride there?"

"Oh Mom, thank you! Yes, I will. I am making an appointment tomorrow and I'll let you know when it is." She left the room and wandered into her bedroom and plopped down on her bed. She surfed the web until bedtime and she slept a fitful sleep with disturbing dreams about dying babies and other morbid things.

****

The next day she had off from school and she slept late. When she got up, she remembered she had to make the phone call to the clinic. She picked up her phone and dialed.

"Hello, Dawson Women's Clinic."

"Um, hello. Um....I need to um...make an appointment for an....um....abortion." Katie pulled a string on her blanket.

"Sure thing. When was your last period?"

"I don't know. I'm irregular but it's been a few months."

"O.k, we would do a sonogram to tell how far along you are. Our prices are based on how far along you are. They start at $350 for 4-5 weeks and go up to $650 for 13-14 weeks. I would bring $650 with you and if you are less, you bring the rest home. We can see you in 4 days on the 25th at 8:00 in the morning. Will you be asking for twilight sleep? If so, bring a ride because you can't drive home after that."

"O.K, Thank you. I will be there."

She hung up the phone and called Derek.

"Hello, Katie."

"Hey. I called the clinic, and they said to bring at least $650 since I am unsure how far along I am. They scheduled me for four days on the 25th at 8:00 in the morning. I talked to my mom, and she is taking me."

"Oh man, how did she take it?"

Katie chewed on her cuticle. "She's disappointed but glad I'm not having it and is supportive of what I am doing."

"That's good. I'm glad she's being supportive, you need that right now. You don't need anyone giving you any shit, you have enough to deal with."

"Yeah, that's true. I'm so conflicted about this. I don't really want to or feel it's right."

"I know Katie. Me too. But we must do it or our lives and this baby's life will be ruined. There's no way around that."

Katie sighed and punched her thigh." I know, I know. My head knows that at least but my heart tells me something else."

"Well, you need to listen to your head. It will make the right decision."

Katie rubbed her eyes. "Yeah, well, I'm tired and need to go to bed. My head hurts with all this information. I will talk to you later."

Katie hung up the phone and got into bed with her clothes on and pulled the covers over her head. She fell asleep quickly but had a fitful sleep with more dreams of dead babies and herself going to hell.

****

Four days passed by faster than Katie wanted them to. She laid in her bed each night and rubbed the hard mound that was on her lower stomach and tried to talk to the baby. She tried to explain why they were doing what they were and that she was so, so sorry and wished it could be different. She cried many tears for the life she was taking and for her own life that she was putting ahead of this baby's life. She kept going back and forth with reasons to stop this and reasons to keep going forward and she kept coming back to thinking the abortion was the best thing, awful as it was. She wanted to become a mother and have a baby but she wanted to do it at the right time for herself and for the baby. She hoped God would let her have this same baby again if she got pregnant again at a future date. She tried to reason with God and make promises to do better and asked Him to please forgive her for what she was doing. The morning came, and she got up at 6:00 and jumped in the shower, and then got dressed. She dressed in an all-black outfit she thought was fitting for the occasion. She heard her mother in the kitchen and walked out. She was queasy and her stomach was churning and she knew she could eat nothing this morning. Her mother looked up when she came in.

"Are you doing O. K? Are you ready for the surgery? I read up on it and it's really quick and easy and you will be just fine. There's a very low complication rate and they say childbirth is more dangerous than a first-trimester abortion. So, don't be worried and get yourself worked up in a frenzy, O.K?"

Katie looked at her mom and said nothing right away. "That's not what's bothering me. If I die or acquire complications, I will be punished for what I am doing. I have feelings for this baby I am getting rid of. That's what I am doing, getting rid of a baby. It's not its fault it got conceived. It's mine and Derek's and now it's getting punished for our mistake."

Katie's mom looked at her with sad eyes. "I understand. I understand this will be hard to do and that it's your baby you are terminating. But, it's early on, and it won't realize anything is happening. You can go on to deliver other babies when the time is right."

Katie didn't wish to be placated with shallow words and promises. Nothing would make this feel right or feel better. They left the house at 7:30 and headed for the clinic. They pulled up to a tan one-story building with several small windows and several larger windows in the front. There was a large tree by the building. They walked up to the door and walked in. Katie walked up to the receptionist and told her she was there. She was given a clipboard with paperwork to fill out, which she took to her seat and did. Soon, she was called in for her sonogram to see how far along she was. She lay on the table and the monitor was turned away from her. She asked to see the screen and was told they do not allow that. Katie wondered why not and was a little annoyed by that because she wanted to see the baby she was killing and say goodbye. The lady told her she was 12 weeks along. She finished and Katie walked out to the receptionist and was told it would cost $550. She handed over the money, feeling like she was paying an executioner or a hitman. She was called into a room and told to remove her clothes and put on a gown, which she did, then she was led to another room with a table in the middle, and the nurse helped her get on and positioned her feet with stirrups.

"Do you want any medication that will make it so you don't experience so much pain?" the nurse asked.

Katie thought about it for a minute. "No, I want to feel it. I owe my baby that much at least."

The nurse looked at her like she was crazy. "Honey, first, there's no baby and second, punishing yourself is not going to change the outcome of the procedure. Are you sure this is what you want to do?"

Katie thought about it again. "Yes, I guess I want it done but I don't want medication."

The nurse shook her head. "Honey, it's gonna hurt, a lot and you can't move around while the doctor is in there. Just know that going into this. You must hold still and you must not scream or yell out and frighten the other patients who aren't being as foolish as you are."

Katie jutted out her chin. "I got it."

She laid back as the doctor came into the room. The nurse told him she was refusing the sedation and the reason why and the doctor just shook his head but proceeded. He stuck the needle in with the numbing mediation into her cervix. Katie bit her lip and took some deep breaths. Then the doctor started dilating her and the cramps came on like a sudden wave.

Katie put her hands over her face and softly moaned. She held perfectly still and took deep breaths in and slow breaths out. Then the doctor got the suction cannula and put it inside of her and turned on the suction machine. Katie's legs and body started vibrating, and she heard a slurping sound and understood it was her baby being sucked out of her. She burst into tears and started sobbing. Great sobs wracked her body as anxiety and emotional agony overtook her. The doctor finished and told her she did a good job and that she wasn't pregnant anymore. *Really, doctor, ya think? Like I don't know that right now, she thought.* They brought her to a room with recliners and had her sit there for an hour. She spent the whole time crying. When it was time to go, she met her mother in the lobby and her mother put her arms around her shoulders. They walked her to the car and they got in and left for home.

"How was it?"

"I refused the sedation, so it hurt a lot and I heard it when it slurped and the baby was sucked into the jar."

"Oh Katie, why did you refuse the sedation? To punish yourself? That wasn't necessary and you shouldn't have been in pain or had to hear that. I don't know what to do with you." She reached over and rubbed Katie's leg.

Katie just stared out the window and watched the world zip by. She saw people living their lives and wondered how many of them killed their babies. She had read that 1 in 3 women will receive an abortion in their lives. *That's a lot of \women, she thought.* She wondered how many of them thought they had killed their babies? She just wanted to die right now and couldn't wait to get home and get into bed. They arrived home and Katie flew into the house and into her room and jumped under her covers, and pulled them over her head. Her mom came in and sat on the edge of the bed and listened to her daughter cry and tried to rub her back but Katie pulled away and curled into a ball. She stayed that way all the next day and into the third until her mother came in and pulled the covers off of her.

"Katie, you must get up and go to school. It's been three days and you're healed, at least physically and you need to get on with your life. That was the whole purpose of getting that done."

Katie ignored her and laid there with her eyes closed and didn't move. Her mother sighed and left the room. When it continued for five days, her mother told her she was bringing her to a doctor. She was going to be seen by a psychiatrist. But Katie couldn't get over the fact that she killed her baby and she couldn't move past the procedure. Her friends were concerned about her and came over.

"Hey girlfriend, how are ya? We missed you in school." Jane said as she pulled the covers off Katie's head.

Katie mumbles something they didn't understand.

Lisa sat down on the bed and rubbed Katie's shoulder. "Katie, it's going to be alright. You didn't do a bad thing. It was the best thing for you, Derek, and the baby. You were strong and made an unselfish decision."

Katie opened her eyes and then narrowed them. "Best for the baby? She's dead. How is being dead, best for her?"

Jane squeezed Katie's shoulder. "You yourself said you didn't want the baby raised in poverty and that is exactly what would've happened if you had it. You, Derek, and the baby would've been miserable and every day would be a fight to survive on minimum wage salaries. The baby would have gone without, maybe even for food. Is that what you would want?"

Katie stared at them. "I could've given her up for adoption. I don't understand why I didn't think of it. No one at the clinic presented that as an option. No one did. She could be alive with parents who could care for her. Why didn't I think of that?"

Jane cocked her head to one side. "Yeah, but how would you know what kind of parents would've gotten her? Even if you picked them out, how would you know what they would really be like? We've all heard horror stories. The baby might've been in a horrific and brutal abuse situation far worse than being dead. Am I right?"

Katie thought about that for a moment. "Yes, but the odds of that are slim. Most people who adopt would do anything for a child and would love and cherish them. Abusers are rare."

"But you never know, Katie. You never know. You could've also died in childbirth. Abortion is much safer than giving birth." Jane said as she raised her eyebrows.

Katie rolled her eyes. "Death by childbirth is exceedingly rare and the odds that it would happen are infinitesimal and it is silly to even say it." She shook her head and started crying.

The girls were running out of encouraging words to say to Katie and she knocked down everything they said.

"Katie, it will get better, I promise. You just need to get past this and move on with your life. You are a good person and nothing will change that. You did nothing to hate yourself for. Please stop beating yourself up." Jane said.

Lisa nodded. "Yeah, Katie, I agree with Jane. Get up and come to school tomorrow. Everyone else misses you. You know our whole group has your back and we'll all be there for you no matter how long it takes. Friends to the end!"

Katie laid back down on the bed and pulled the covers back over her face, the girls looked at each other with sad expressions and got up and left the room. Katie continued to cry until she cried herself to sleep.

****

Two days later, nothing was better with Katie and she saw a psychiatrist who prescribed her an antidepressant and an anti-anxiety medication. He gave her a thirty-day supply and said to come back in 30 days. Katie had an appointment with a counselor but the soonest they could get her in was three weeks. Her mom filled the prescriptions and took her home. When they got into the kitchen, she gave Katie the first of the pills and put the pill bottles on the shelf. Katie wandered to her room and slid back under her covers and stayed there the rest of the day. Her mother managed to get her to eat some food, but it was not as much as she really needed, so she left her alone. Katie waited until her mom was asleep and strode into the kitchen and grabbed the medicine bottles and a glass of water and poured the pills into her hand. She swallowed multiple pills at one time until both bottles were in her stomach. She left the bottles on the counter and walked back to her room and dove under the covers. She closed her eyes and waited and soon she was very groggy. Soon the room spun around and her breathing became labored, then she slowly lost consciousness with her hands rested over her chest.

****

The next morning, Katie's mom tottered into the kitchen half-asleep, looking to make her morning coffee. She started the coffee in the machine and glanced over at the pill bottles on the counter. She wondered if Katie got up and took her morning dose so she walked over and picked up the bottles. To her horror, both bottles were empty. She dropped the bottles and ran into Katie's bedroom and grabbed Katie by the shoulders.

"Katie, wake up. Please wake up. For the love of God, wake up." Then she touched Katie's face, which was ice cold.

She ran to the phone and called 911 and came back to the room. She told the police her daughter wasn't breathing, and she was going to do CPR and gave them her address. She pushed on Katie's chest and blew air into her mouth, but she understood it was futile because of how cold Katie's skin was and the blue pallor to her lips.

"Oh Katie, why did you do this? Oh God, why did I encourage her to abort when I knew she did not want to? Why?"

Katie was laid to rest on a cold, rainy morning and all her friends and family were there. Many blamed themselves for what happened and everyone wished they could've done more. All lamented the total waste of a beautiful life.

Rebecca had tears running down her face when she realized how badly this would have turned out if she had not intervened in Katie's life.

Then she was shown another scene.

CHAPTER NINE

J amal was out on his usual route to sell his quota of drugs. He had crack, heroin, and meth to sell today. He normally only sold one type at a time but Rocco wanted more products moved and felt this was the way to do it. He put his stash in the pockets of his black jean jacket, each drug with its own pocket and he grabbed his baseball cap and put it on backward, and headed out the door. He found Tyrell, a twelve-year-old boy, who was going to be his lookout today, sitting on his front steps waiting for him. Tyrell was small for his age and had delicate features. His brown skin glowed and his big brown puppy dog eye's always looked like he was pleading for something. His short black hair was cut close to his scalp and a lightning bolt was etched into the back. His ears stuck out and were pierced in one lobe with a fake diamond stud. He wore loose black jeans, pulled down low, and an oversized black hoodie.

"Hey, Ty, let's get rollin, we have lotsa ground to cover today and more product to sell than normal. Get yo head out of yo ass and be on guard, got it?"

Tyrell rolled his eyes and shrugged his shoulders. "Yeah, Yeah, don't I always? Get off my back asswipe, unless I'm not doin what I'm spose to do."

Jamal smacked him on the back of the head. "Watch yo mouth boy, don't give me any backtalk, ya feel me?"

Tyrell gave him a dirty look and ducked in case he got hit again. They walked to Pennyroyal Street and Tyrell took his spot on the corner. Jamal walked slowly up and down the street. Every so often, someone would stop him.

"Got smack?" And Jamal would pocket the money and discreetly pass the packet of heroin into the person's hand.

Another person approached him, a skinny white girl, made up of more bones than flesh. "Got some rock?" And Jamal discreetly grabbed the money and passed the crack to her. He saw several of his regulars and he knew exactly what they wanted. A small Hispanic girl, barely five foot, and also more bones than flesh came for her usual multiple bags of meth. Suddenly there was a shout and Tyrell yelled "Fuzz", their codeword for the police. Jamal looked around and saw a police car come riding down the road. He put his hands in his pockets and continued to stroll nonchalantly down the road. Then Tyrell yelled. 'They gone." And he got back down to business. He and Tyrell walked around the block to Parson's Street, which was teeming with more people. Tyrell kept his eyes open for the police by walking to the end of the street where there was a stop sign and he could see the cars coming from multiple directions. A tall white man, skinny as a skeleton in ripped jeans, and a soiled white t-shirt came up to Jamal.

"Hey Jamal, can you spot me two ten bags? I'm getting money tonight. I need a taste now, desperately. Please!"

Jamal looked him over. "Hey man, you owe me $40 still so I ain't spottin you more."

The man furrowed his eyebrows, which were dripping with sweat, and put his palms together and held them up to Jamal. "Please man, I'm desperate. I'm getting sick. I just need a taste."

Jamal pursed his lips. "Listen fool. I give it to you and I don't get it ALL back next time I'm seein you, I gonna kick yo ass, ya hear?"

The man closed his eyes. "Thank you, man, thank you. I won't let you down." And he took the two packets from Jamal.

"You bet yo ass you won't. I ain't playin here." Jamal said.

Then Jamal and Tyrell headed to the next block, nearby a park and playground. There was the sound of the kids shouting and laughing. Tyrell stood by the corner and watched. Jamal met a customer by the entrance to the playground.

"Got smack?" A tall, gangly young looking man asked him.

"HEY! YOU! There are children here. Peddle your crap somewhere else, not in front of a playground, you hear me, young man?"

Jamal jumped and spun around and there was a lady standing there with her hands on her hips."

"You just mind yo business bitch, this don't concern you."

"These children ARE my business and don't you call me a bitch, my name is Rebecca and you will address me as such."

Jamal was taken aback by this brave woman, few would dare stand up to him and this intrigued him.

"Take your poison and peddle it somewhere else, or better yet, not at all." She said as she stood there with her hands on her hips. "Why don't you get a real job that doesn't hurt people? And stop using children as your look-outs, I can see the boy up there is watching us intently. Aren't you worried about the fact that drug dealers have shorter lifespans and the same goes for gangsta life?"

Jamal just stared at her and couldn't think of a good comeback. "Well, I do all right for myself, REBECCA."

Rebecca smirked at him. "It may seem that way for the moment but things can change in an instant. Someone desperate for drugs could stab you or shoot you to get your stash."

It was Jamal's turn to smirk back at her. "I have my protection." He brought out a switchblade and opened it for a moment, and then closed it. Then he pulled a gun from his waist and briefly flashed it to her."No one's gonna rob me. They know they gonna see their maker if they do."

"And they can't surprise you? Are YOU ready to meet your maker?" Rebecca cocked her head to one side.

Jamal thought about that for a moment. "My maker ain't gonna be too happy to see me, I guess."

Rebecca took her arms and folded them over her chest. "That's something to really think about, isn't it? "

Jamal was uncomfortable talking to this lady and talking about this topic. "I'll go to another block away from the park. I ain't got too many customers here anyway."

Rebecca nodded her head. "Good, and think about the things I said. I'm willing to talk to you anytime and even find you a real job."

Jamal stared at her for a moment and then turned around and walked away. He decided to go down Goodwell Street and Tyrell followed him close behind. Jamal looked back at the boy and had some uncomfortable thoughts about what he was doing. *Damn, that lady got to me, he thought.* He pushed them aside and started looking for customers. He didn't have long to wait.

A disheveled, dirty man, who was seriously underweight approached him. "Meth, man. Need meth. Give me a gram."

Jamal produced the packets and discreetly handed the man the drugs while at the same time taking the money. Suddenly Tyrel yelled "Fuzz" and he took his hands out of his pockets and strolled down the street. A Police cruiser slowly made its way down the street and Jamal did not glance up at the car and pretended to check out his phone. The cop car left, and he went back to selling mode.

He kept selling until 10:00 at night and walked with Tyrell back to their homes. Tyrell lived in the same apartment building as he did. He stopped and pulled out two twenties and a ten and gave Tyrell fifty dollars. That was a lot of money for a twelve-year-old in this neighborhood and to make it in just one night. Tyrell worked with him four days a week, which gave him $200 a week. Being a lookout was a job many of the young boys in the neighborhood aspired to be. He had another boy, Lemarcus, that he used the other three days a week. He was thirteen years old. He walked up the stairs to his apartment and threw his coat down. He took his money and placed it on the table to count. It came to $2200, not a bad haul for the night. He got ready for bed and when he was lying down, he thought of that woman, Rebecca, and the things that she said. They gave him disturbing thoughts that he took to sleep with him. He tossed and turned and had a night of troubling dreams.

****

Jamal slept late and got up at 11:00. He showered and dressed for the day and ate some cereal for breakfast. He surfed the web for a while and then watched TV until 3:00. Then it was time to go out again to sell his stash. He waited on the steps for Lemarcus to show up and grew impatient waiting there for him. Soon, a boy, about five feet tall, with ebony-colored skin and dyed light brown hair in ringlets all over his head. He was wearing blue jeans that were hanging low enough to see his boxers and a blue and grey hoodie that was pulled up over his head. His hair ringlets stuck out the front.

"Where ya been, boy? I been waiten for twenty minutes. Time is money boy and do you want it to come out of yo pay, huh? Ya here? Don't be a fool."

Lemarcus jutted out his lip and narrowed his eyes. "I been doin homework, man. Ya here? I don't wanna be doin this shit the rest of my sorry life."

'Well, yo life will be sorry if ya keep me waiten again like that or I find someone else who pays their due respect to me. You boys want yo money, but don't respect the work to get it." Jamal reached out and smacked Lemarcus on the back of his head.

'Yo man, don't ya be doin that again, ya hear? I gots me some self-respect." Lemarcus rubbed the back of his head.

"That's why younger boys under teen years are better for the business. They pay me the respect I deserve. " Jamal mumbled under his breath. "And get no jail time."

They walked down the street and crossed over and Jamal started selling his goods. He didn't have long to wait.

"Yo man, got smack? $100 worth?" A skinny girl who looked no more than sixteen dressed in ripped jeans and a stained white and black striped shirt said.

Jamal reached into his pocket and got out the bags and then discreetly passed them to her and grabbed the money in one stealthy pass. He pocketed the money and continued selling. Soon his stash was depleted, and he walked up to Lemarcus to grab some more. He had the boys hold much of the stash so if he was caught he would not have so much on him. The boys rarely got more than a slap on the wrist when they were under twelve years old. He was thinking Lemarcus was getting too old for this at age thirteen. Oddly, he did care about the boys and tried to be a father figure to them, since so many lacked that. He was looked up to by the kids in the neighborhood for his flashy money, flashy clothes, and his expensive jewelry. He also had a flashy car that he liked to tour the streets with and would give the kids rides. He also bought the kids ice cream and little trinkets when he was in a good mood. He had a girlfriend, Latoya, who was beautiful and quite fine. She was thin but had a shapely butt and her brown hair with golden highlights hair hung down her back in tight spiral curls. Her skin was light brown and smooth and she had a delicate nose and luscious pink lips. She dressed in beautiful stylish clothes that Jamal bought for her and fine jewelry that he would surprise her with. He wanted a fine-looking woman by his side.

They got close to the playground and Jamal wondered if Rebecca was there. She was a pain in the ass but she intrigued him and made him want to know more about her. They were at the edge of the playground and he got a customer.

A tall, white, deathly pale and emaciated woman approached him. She was skin and bones and had sores all over her face and her facial bones stood out oddly. She had the classic appearance of a meth user so Jamal knew what she wanted before she asked. He winced when she got close and a tinge of shame filled him, knowing his drugs were disfiguring her and would probably ultimately kill her if she didn't stop.

"Hey, give me $200 worth. Can you give me extra since I am buying so much?" She asked.

Jamal looked at her and nodded. "I'll give you two extra bags." Then they quickly made the deal.

Then he turned around, and he almost jumped out of his skin. Rebecca was standing directly behind him and he had not heard or seen her walk up.

"Can't you see what your drugs are doing to that woman? Even if she stops, she will be disfigured for life and if she doesn't stop, she'll be dead in six months, if that long."

Jamal started speaking and stuttering. "Um, well, um.....If I ...don't get them to her....um..she'll get them...um from ....um someone...um..else."

"But then you would not be responsible for her and you would be absolved of her addiction and if she died from the drugs, you would not be partially responsible." She put her hand on her hip.

Jamal fidgeted with his hands. "Yeah, true that I guess." He hated that she was right.

"If you keep doing this, you will keep adding bodies to your count. And when you stand before God you will have to answer for them. Do you want to stand before God the way you are now if you were to die today?"

Jamal's body squirmed. He wanted to tell this woman to go to hell, yet what she was saying had meaning. "I don't wanna stand fore God like this and I sure don't wanna go to hell."

Rebecca nodded and reached out and put a hand on his shoulder. "Would you go with me to get something to eat?"

Jamal couldn't believe what he was about to say. "Yeah sure enough."

Jamal called to Lemarcus. "Hey boy, I won't be needin ya right now, today. I'll let ya know when I be needin ya again."

He followed Rebecca down the street to a diner and they walked in and found a booth. They sat across from each other.

"Jamal, what would you say if I found you a real job? It wouldn't be glamourous but it would pay the bills and leave you with some extra. You wouldn't have the thousands you have now or a glamorous lifestyle but it would be respectable. You would work in my father's business as a sort of gopher and do odd jobs and tasks and bring mail to people and files. Once you do well at that, we could see about doing something more challenging, with better pay." Rebecca cocked her head to one side and raised her eyebrows.

Jamal looked up at the ceiling. Why the hell was he even considering this? It would be a major downgrade in his lifestyle and his girlfriend would not be happy. But he was drawn to this woman and her concern for his life. He made a decision that stunned him.

"I guess I could give it a try. No harm in that, I'm guessin. What do I have to wear?"

Rebecca smiled. "You could wear a polo shirt and Docker style pants."

"I'd look like a freak. A white boy, goody two shoes, man. Oh, man.......I guess I can do it cuz there ain't nuthin I can't do." He jutted out his chin when he said that.

"Here's the address. Be there at 9:00 in the morning tomorrow and I will let my dad know you are coming." She wrote down the address and her phone number and handed it to him.

He took it and looked at it. It was uptown probably ten minutes away, and he knew how to get there.

"I be there tomorrow, I will. I got nuthin to lose I guess to try this white boy, pansy job."

Rebecca smiled and held out her hand to him. He looked at it for a minute and then reached out his hand and shook hers. *At least with this job I ain't makin a deal with the devil, he thought.*

****

The next day Jamal dressed in the light blue polo shirt and Docker pants he had bought and he wore a tan pair of loafers. He thought he looked like a freak, a white pansy goody two shoe boy. He walked out to his car and followed the directions to a large white three-story office building. He hurried into the reception area and told the receptionist he was there. Five minutes later a tall, stately-looking man dressed in a business suit came walking out.

"Hi, you must be Jamal. I'm Rebecca's father, Todd. Come with me and I will show you what you will be doing. I am going to have you work in my office and you will be my gopher, to put it one way. I will also have you make trips to the mailroom and you will deliver the mail. And then when something needs to be sent to another department, you will do that. My secretary will show you how to file papers in the drawers. You will also go down to pick up and food the staff order for their lunches. We'll keep you busy so you don't get bored. Payday is every Friday and since today is Monday, I will make sure you get a paycheck this week so you don't have to wait two weeks. I'm sure you will do well. My daughter seems to have a lot of faith in you."

Jamal did what he was asked, and the day passed by quickly. By the time 5:00 came, he had felt more at home. Everyone was so nice and kind to him and did not treat him like a thug. The rest of the week also passed by quickly and Friday came and he got his paycheck. He groaned because he usually made a lot more than that in just one day selling his drugs. He decided he would sell his flashy car and get something more reasonable so the insurance rates would be lower. He was glad he had stayed in his rent-controlled apartment so he could afford it on this salary. It had been his grandmother's apartment, and it got passed down to him when she died. When he got home, a bunch of the young boys had gathered on the stoop of his apartment building.

"Hey man, why ya lookin so stuffy now?" One of the boys asked.

"Man, you don't look so cool no more. You goin straight now?" Another asked.

Jamal decided he would explain to the boys why he made such drastic changes and maybe, just maybe, he could steer them away from the thug life.

"I didn't want to sell no drugs that could kill people. It would be on my soul if each one up and died, and it ruins their life and health. Man, drugs kill......Um...Do you want it on yo conscience if you kill someone? Hey

Jerome, you could get a job at a store. You don't have to run drugs or start to sell them. Jameel, you could deliver papers."

"But man, the money sucks, Jamal. I could make big money doin it. Why work at a job that pays peanuts?"

"Because ya'll gotta live with yo self. Is money worth a dirty and shitty conscience? Is it worth riskin jail time? Yo, ya'll wanna to risk spendin years in a rough jail? Ya'll wanna risk gettin shot at? Dyin at a young age?" Jamal spread his hands out to everyone.

****

Several months passed and Jamal had an idea. There wasn't much for the youngsters to do after school, most had no daddies and many had one or more parents on drugs. There was an empty warehouse down the road. It was big enough for a basketball court. And to put in games, a pool table, foosball and other fun stuff for kids to do. He decided he would approach Rebecca's father and ask if he would sponsor building a community center. He would also go to all the businesses in the area and get them involved and try to get more men and women involved to mentor the kids.

His idea took flight, and the businesses were thrilled to get the kids off the street. Men and women volunteered to help and Rebecca's father bought the warehouse. Companies donated resources to fix it up and donated the games and activities that would keep the kids busy. The basketball court was paid for by an NBA All-Star who had lived in the area as a child and he came in and gave the kids pointers and advice on playing.

Jamal's girlfriend left him for a drug dealer who could keep her in the lifestyle she was used to. Jamal lamented it for a while and realized she was with him for his money. He met another woman who was coming in there to be a mentor and they hit it off right away. She was 26 and Jamal was 23 and she worked as a pediatric nurse in the children's hospital. Jamal and Latisha became the de facto parents for many of the kids at the center. Then when they married they were surprised with a little one of their own. Three of them to be exact, two girls and a boy, Jamal Jr, and the twins, LaVerna and LaDonna. Rebecca came and visited the center every so often and encouraged Jamal and Latisha in their efforts and they made Rebecca their children's godmother. Then Jamal started a community watch program to stay on top of the drug and violence situation in the community. Neighbors throughout the community took part and crime went down one hundredfold. Everyone took an interest in their community and got it cleaned up when it came to crime and when it came to garbage on the streets. They cleaned up the needles all over the ground and chased the drug dealers off the streets and made it safer for the children. No one had to worry about drug dealers in front of the park anymore. Jamal also started up a Big Brother and Big Sister program and found no shortage of volunteers in the community. Many former drug dealers and addicts in recovery even volunteered. One of Jamal's former customers came to see him. It was Roberta and she wanted off the drugs. With Rebecca's help, Jamal got her into a fantastic rehab. She finished the program and came back to thank Jamal and Rebecca and to volunteer her time to help others. She spoke at many events and she mentored many young people who were on drugs and wanted off them and also kids who had never touched the stuff yet. She came today to talk to Jamal.

"Hey, Jamal. I want to thank you for all you've done for me and my kids. You started out as my dealer and then saved me from the drugs. Thank you and God bless you!"

Jamal smiled and squirmed. He wasn't used to all the compliments he gets now. "Yo welcome Roberta. It still makes me hot and bothered knowing I could've helped kill you."

Roberta reached out and gave him a hug. "It's what matters now. Definitely, what matters now and that is very good." They pulled away and Roberta went on her way.

Jamal's two lookouts, Tyrell and Lemarcus, continued to admire and look up to him and they both got respectable jobs with Jamal's help. Rebecca even became a Big Sister to two girls, twelve-year-old Lucrecia, and thirteen-year-old, Dominique and she met with them for an hour and gave them two fifteen-minute phone calls every week. And she was working on an open adoption plan with Domonique who was five months pregnant with twins so Jamal and Latisha could adopt her babies. Jamal was excited and nervous to soon be a father of a 3-year-old, 1-year-old, and two newborns in 5 months. Today was a big day. Jamal and Latisha were receiving an award for everything they have done for the community and they were also celebrating five years of opening the community center. Jamal looked back and couldn't believe all that has happened in the past five years and how far he had come, from drug dealer to office worker and community leader, he has accomplished what many would view as impossible and he knew it was due to two people. One was God and the other was Rebecca. If she had not taken an interest in him and offered him a job, he shuddered at the thought of where he would be today. A very good possibility was dead and, or at least causing the death of others. Now he has redeemed himself of his troubled past and he was excited to see how the future would unfold.

Rebecca had tears in her eyes as she watched the memories unfold before her eyes. Jesus then let another scene unfold, much different than the one before.

CHAPTER TEN

Jamal woke up at 11:00 and jumped into the shower. Twenty minutes later he was dressed and ready to start his day. He had a lot of product to sell and it wasn't going to sell itself. He grabbed the bag with packets of heroin and the bag with packets of meth and a smaller bag with a packet of crack and put them in his jacket that had many pockets. Then he waited on the stoop for Tyrell. The boy was late again, and he was in no mood for it.

Then he saw the twelve-year-old boy come ambling down the road. "Hurry up boy, if ya know what's good for ya. I'm tired of always waiten for ya. You wanna not get paid?"

Tyrell rolled his eyes, which bought him a slap on the back of his head. "Ouch! Hey, man. You don't wanna be hitten me fo sure."

" Don't be sassing me, if yo know what's good fo yo. "He reached out to slap the boy again but the boy ducked and missed getting hit.

"O. K., O. K, I won't be sassing ya, fo sure."

Jamal started walking, with Tyrell following him. "We be goin to Randall Street first. Get at yo post." The boy ran ahead and positioned himself at the corner.

Jamal didn't have too long to wait for his first customer. A thin, emaciated woman with facial bones that jutted out approached him. He could tell by her facial disfigurements what her drug of choice was and knew her name, Roberta. "Gimme $120." She said. He reached in his coat and brought out the packets and, with one expert gesture handed her the drugs and took the money.

"Hey, that's not enough for $120." She said.

"Roberta, Ya know I don't skim people, so dontcha try it," Jamal said, and he narrowed his eyes.

"I pay you enough you should give me extra," Roberta said as she pocketed the packs of powder.

Jamal smirked. "I gotta business here, can't be given away product all the time. I give you extra many times, so don't even."

Roberta grunted. "Yeah, whatever." And she hurried on her way.

His next customer was a tall, skinny white guy, at least six foot four. He had no meat on his body and his hair hung in greasy strands down his back and his pants were ripped and his shirt stained. "Gimme $40."

Jamal made the exchange quickly and moved onto the street with the playground. He was stopped by the entranceway by a gaunt-faced man, dressed in dirty shorts and a ripped and stained yellow shirt. "$60" Jamal felt around in his bag and pulled out the baggies. Just then a ball bounced off their feet and a child, no more than six came running to get it. Jamal stopped the ball with his foot and kicked it over to the kid.

"Hey, thanks, guy!" The kid said as he grabbed the ball and ran back into the park.

Jamal finished the transaction, and the man moved on. Suddenly he heard Tyrell yell "Fuzz!" And he put his hands in his pockets and pretended to be looking for someone in the park. The police car cruised down the street slowly and almost stopped when it got to the park. Jamal took a few steps into the park and sat down on a bench and watched the police car drive by. They had regular patrols in the area but rarely arrested anyone. He looked over and by a tree, there was the man who bought from him shooting up heroin, in full view of the parents and children in the park. Then he dropped his needle on the ground and got up and left. Jamal stared at the spot where he dropped the needle and then looked around at all the kids in the park. Finally, he shrugged his shoulders and rose up to begin his sales. *It ain't my job to clean up after the junkies but they shouldn't be doing it in the park and dumping their needles there, he reasoned.*

Another person from the park approached him. A short, heavy-set woman with short blonde hair and acne covering her face. She wore clean untorn clothes. She asked him for $20 of crack, which he found by rummaging in his pocket for the bag that contained it He brought out four small baggies and handed it to her, and pocketed the $20.

He finished at 9:00 at night and headed home. Tyrell continued on to his apartment building just a few places down and Jamal walked up the three flights of stairs to his apartment. He took out what little was left of his stash from his pockets and took the money and put it in a pile on the table. He sat down and counted his money. $1800 and that made him smile. It wasn't the most he made in one day but it was also nothing to sneeze at either. He laid down in his bed and wandered off to sleep.

****

A week later, Jamal got up late. He had slept until noon and when he saw the time, he rushed into the bathroom to have his shower. He got dressed in a pair of designer jeans and a Calvin Klein shirt. He put on his $250 pair of black and red Air Jordon sneakers and gathered his stash for the day and put them in the pockets of his jacket. He hurried out to the steps of his building and waited for his lookout, Lamarcus to show up. *Damn, these kids don't take their jobs seriously but they liked the money, he thought.* Lamarcus showed up, wandering down the street.

"Hurry yo ass boy, time is money and you be losing it soon if yo ass keep bein late and keepin me waitin."

Lamarcus just shrugged his shoulders, which earned him a slap on the back of the head. Jamal enjoyed doing that to those who make him mad. They walked down to Trenton Street and Jamal got to work. It didn't take long and Roberta came up to him.

"Need $80 now. The stuff you gave me yesterday was the dope. Good stuff. But do you have the kickin dope that's been going around? I heard the black tar stuff is potent and an amazing high. If ya got it, I want that."

Jamal nodded. "I gots the super pure high grade stuff this week so yo gettin yo money worth."

Roberta gave him the money, and he passed her the heroin.

****

Roberta took the heroin and put it in her pocket. She walked down to her apartment building and rushed up the stairs. She hurried into her apartment and into her bathroom. She got out her works, a spoon, a lighter, a strip of rubber, and a syringe. She hated doing this to herself and that's why she preferred smoking meth but she wanted a taste of this good stuff that has been going down the rumor mill. She took the rubber and tied it around her upper arm really tight. Then she looked for a vein. She was having trouble locating a decent one. Her arms were covered in scabs from the meth and she had used heroin enough times to have scar tissue in her veins. They also like to play hide and seek on her. She thought she spotted one and plunged the needle in. She pulled back on the plunger and nothing, no red blood. *DAMN! I missed. This is gonna be hard, she thought.* She stuck the needle into the vein higher up and again pulled back the plunger and again nothing. *Oh shit, this is gonna be miserable. The high better be worth it, she thought.* She looks for another vein and still has no luck. She takes off the rubber and puts it on her other arm and ties it as tight as she can and searches for a vein. She sees one possibility and goes for it. The needle goes in and she winces. The plunger gets pulled back and again, no blood. She was shaking now with nerves and the need to get a drug into her system. *Please, let me get this right this time.* She takes it off and puts it around her ankle. It hurts like hell to do it in your foot or ankle but at this point, she did not care. She saw one plump and juicy vein pop up. She guided the needle in and pulled back the plunger. *RED BLOOD! SHE GOT IT!* She then pushes the plunger down and watches the liquid go into her vein. Within seconds she feels warm all over and a rush and high so amazing that she can't believe it. But then everything started getting fuzzy. She felt herself drifting off and fought to keep her eyes open. She was paralyzed to her spot and couldn't move. Breathing was becoming labored and slowing down, as was her pulse and blood pressure. Her last thought was. *Damn, I think this stuff is too good. I think I'm overdosing.* And then she faded into unconsciousness and slouched over. She fell to her side on the floor. Her breathing became shallower and shallower until it was almost undetectable. And then her brain told her body to stop breathing and her heartbeat stopped from lack of oxygen. That was how her two children, nine-year-old Janelle and seven-year-old, Marcus found her when they came home from school.

****

Jamal woke up excited. Today, he was going to make a huge purchase of heroin and meth. It was going to be enough that he could hire dealers. He actually was going to have his own network and posse. He was on his way to being a kingpin in his neighborhood and he couldn't be happier. He got on his phone and called his friends to see who wanted to work for him. This would mean more dealers on the street, more drugs, and more money going into his pocket. He called his friend Jaquon.

"Hey man, how's it hanging?" Jamal asked.

"It's all good." Jaquon said.

Jamal decided to get right to the point. "I'm lookin fo dealers to be workin fo me. There be the possibility of grabbin over $1000 a week,"

"Fo sure? I want in on it."

"O. K. man, I be hookin you up with the drugs so come here today."

Jamal hung up and dialed his friend D'Qann.

"Hey man. Wanna make yoself some easy cash?"

"'Fo sure I would. Is it dealin? If it is, then I be in it," "

"Yeah, it is. Come to my apartment to get yo stash."

Jamal hung up feeling good and satisfied with himself. He got the drugs packed up in big bags and wrote his friends' names on them. Then he wrote in a book exactly what he gave them and exactly what he should get back when they were done minus their cut. His smile couldn't be bigger. He was moving up in the world. He also wrote down the streets in his territory and wrote some streets he wanted to add to it. He knew he was close to Kameel's territory and Kameel did not tolerate anyone cutting into his turf. When he was done sorting and packing, he realized he needed another dealer so he called his friend Jackson. He too wanted in on the enterprise so Jamal had three dealers under him but he wanted more. He wanted to be THE source for drugs on the Southside. Soon, his friends arrived, and he gave them the lowdown on dealing. He also made sure they knew that he knew how much they had in their stash and that he would be keeping a close eye on the money coming back. He won't take cutting the product or skimming from it so easy. *They are my friends, but this was money, and money is always kept separate from friendship, he thought.*

****

The Southside wasn't the best place, to begin with, but soon the drug problem escalated to a point where there seemed no return. Addicts increased the crime rate and having your home broken into was the norm. Needles were scattered everywhere and as fast as the town tried to clean them up, they kept multiplying. The powers that be also decided to do a needle exchange, which greatly increased the number on the streets. Overdoses happened daily and paramedics, as well as the police, carried the drug overdose reversal medication naloxone on them at all times. Parents were afraid to let their kids play outside and there were random drive-by shootings weekly. They resulted from turf wars over the distribution of the drugs. People who had the means moved away from the area and the ones that stayed lived in fear daily. The little boys biggest dreams and aspirations were to be a lookout and when they were older a full-fledged drug dealer.

Little girls learned to look up to these men, and they wanted all the good things in life that drug money could buy, but they also had to live in the fear of being raped, which also was a daily occurrence.

****

Jamal fulfilled his dream and became the number one dealer in the area, he had twelve dealers under him and that was still growing. But the dealers he took territory from were grumbling amongst themselves and wanted to get rid of Jamal and his enterprise. They wanted their territories back and were willing to do anything it took to get that. Kameel was Jamal's number one enemy and Jamal decided to hire security for himself and his girlfriend. His girlfriend was a spoiled, self-indulged woman that was after his money and not his love. But she was beautiful and had a body any runway model would envy so she was good eye-candy hanging onto Jamal's arm.

Today he was taking Tanisha out to a fancy restaurant uptown. They were celebrating Tanisha's pregnancy. They exited their apartment and descended the stairs. Then a car roared by and shots rang out. Tanisha was hit in the head and died instantly, the baby with her. Jamal was shot in the stomach, shoulder, and leg. He collapsed to the ground in agonizing pain. He looked over to see Tanisha, but she lay there lifeless, with her eyes half opened, with a bullet hole above her right eye. Jamal felt the blood leaving his body and pooling onto the pavement. His life flashed through his eyes and he realized that he did not lead an exemplary life and had harmed many people, but it was too late to go back and change things. He was terrified of dying, not knowing where he was going. *I am going to hell, he thought.* And that was the last thought he had before closing his eyes and taking his last breath.

Rebecca watched this with wide eyes and she was so glad she intervened in this man's life. The consequences of her not doing so was staggering. She had almost single-handedly saved a town and its people by helping one solitary person.

CHAPTER ELEVEN

Sally woke up to voices in the living room fighting and yelling and she got up to investigate. She walked into the living room and her twins were each pulling on each end of the T.V remote.

"I had it first," Morgan yelled.

"No, I had it first. You always get to pick what's on T.V." Megan yelled and she pulled extra hard and the remote slipped out of Morgan's hand and she went flying back onto the ground with a BANG."Ouch! My back hurts now, you jerk."

Megan and Morgan were identical twins and had beautiful strawberry blonde hair that flowed down their backs in long ringlets. Their eyes were huge light blue spheres with strawberry blond eyelashes and below was a small pug nose. Their skin was pale, almost translucent, and had a smattering of reddish freckles across their noses and cheeks. They will be turning seven years old in a few days. Just then, two little tow-headed boys came tottering into the living room. Their sisters yelling woke them up. They had wide blue eyes like their sisters and the same white, translucent skin. Toby's blonde hair was straight as a pin and was cut in a bowl cut. Lucas's hair was a tousle of blonde curls that were unruly and hard to tame. Toby was five years old and had a birthday several weeks ago. Lucas was three and a half years old and still was in his terrible two's. They sat down on the couch and Sally found a T.V show they all agreed upon. There was a cry from the bedroom and Sally rushed in to find her two-year-old toddler standing in her crib. She had blonde hair too, but it was baby fine and thin and barely covered her head. She had ice blue eyes and a small pug nose and her skin was a pale, creamy color with rosy cheeks. Her eyes were an oriental shape, with heavily hooded eyelids and a large tongue that sometimes stuck out of her mouth, which made her drool excessively. Marissa had Down Syndrome. Sally picked her up and brought her to the living room and sat her in her little bean bag chair. Marissa stood up and cried and took a few tottering steps and fell to the ground. She picked herself up and took a few more tottering steps and grabbed some books from the bookcase and sat down hard on her diapered behind. Marissa had recently started walking the past few weeks even though her peers were walking for a year or so now. Sally walked into the kitchen and looked through the cabinets for food to feed her children. She stood there and stared for a while at the empty and bare shelves. There was a half-empty box of generic Cheerios, so she grabbed that. She opened the fridge and pulled out a half-empty bottle of apple juice. She grabbed the milk bottle and shook it. It only had a quarter of the milk left, not enough for four children. Thankfully, she still nursed Marissa, so she didn't need to worry about milk for her. She put the cereal in bowls and it was barely enough for the four of them to receive a small bowl. She dripped the milk out of the bottle over each of the bowls and it barely made the cereal wet. She had an eight ounce bottle of expressed breast milk and she used that in their cereal. She would nurse Marissa after she ate her dry cereal. She called the children to the table, and they came running in a stampede into the kitchen and took their seats. Megan took one look at the bowl and frowned.

"Mommy, there's not enough milk in here. I can barely see it."

Sally sighed. "I'm sorry Megan, it's all we have and we must make do."

Sally did not mention to her that she was going to go without breakfast that morning so her kids could eat. Megan didn't like that answer.

"We never have enough food. It's not fair. We don't get any fun foods or any cereals that I like. I want to go to school because we get a good breakfast and lunch there."

Sally was grateful for the school. Her kids got free breakfast and lunch and she didn't know what she would do without that.

"I'm sorry, sweetie, Mommy is doing the best she can. My job doesn't pay much and we need to pay a lot of bills."

"It's not fair Mommy, why can't we have more money like other people have? We never get anything good." Megan said, as she stuck out her bottom lip and frowned.

Sally sighed and closed her eyes. "I don't know Megan. I just don't know." Sally wanted to add that their father didn't give them much money, and she was doing most of it all on her own.

The children ate their cereal with much groaning and complaining and when they were done, Sally cleaned up their bowls and spoons. She wondered what she was going to feed them for lunch and dinner. She looked through the cabinets and refrigerator and came up with half a loaf of bread and an almost empty bottle of peanut butter and an almost empty bottle of Jelly. For dinner, she found a box of macaroni and cheese. She hoped she could stretch the box to feed all five kids, and she understood she could not get any herself. She looked again for something for herself to eat and found a can of sweet potatoes and a can of asparagus. She realized the kids wouldn't eat that, so she opened them up and heated them in the microwave. She got her hot food and sat down at the table and ate them. She cared little for the asparagus but she loved the sweet potatoes and she put a little cinnamon and sugar on them. When she was finished, she looked in her wallet to see how much money she had and she counted $25.69. She could not get food stamps because she wasn't officially separated from her husband and they used his salary to determine if they qualify. She wondered what she could get for that. She loaded the kids up in the van and she was grateful she had filled the gas tank a few days ago. They arrived at Aldi's supermarket and she parked the car. The kids got out, and she got the baby out and they walked in. She walked to the dinner section and got some boxes of macaroni and cheese, and Ramen noodles. Then she walked to the cereal section and grabbed two boxes of cereal. She got a big box of corn flakes and a box of generic cheerio's..She also picked out one box of sweetened cereal. The kids ran up and down the aisle looking at all the cereal.

"Mommy, I want cereal with marshmallows in it. This one, this one!" Megan said as she grabbed a box of cereal. "I don't want corn flakes, get this one instead."

"Megan, that box is small and the corn flakes are twice the size and it cost less than the box with marshmallows in it. I need to get the biggest boxes we can get, so they last. I got this box of fruit loops as a sweet cereal for you guys."

Megan pouted and stamped her foot. "I want this one. THIS one tastes better than yucky old corn flakes."

Sally closed her eyes and sighed. "Megan, I'm sorry. I must get the most for the money I have. I don't get paid for five days. And even with that, most must go to bills."

Megan started to cry. "It's not fair. We don't get good food and we need to eat the same old yucky stuff."

Sally didn't notice the lady standing at the end of the aisle, listening to them.

"I'm sorry Megan. I have to get the food that's going to last us the longest. Come on, let's go get some milk."

They walked to the dairy section, and she grabbed a gallon of whole milk. She groaned at the price of it. She saw that eggs were marked down to $.79 a dozen, and she grabbed one. She wished the kids didn't have off from school. She looked at what was in the cart. She didn't know how they were going to make do. She tried to add up the things in her head and realized they could only get a few more things. She decided to get another 2 packages of Ramen noodles which were a 12-pack for $1.49, and another four boxes of macaroni and cheese which were two boxes for $1.00. Then she walked to the cereal section again and got another box of corn flakes that was $1.29 for a big box. She grabbed 2 bags of lentils and 3 cans of mixed vegetables and 2 containers of chicken broth and a bag of rice. She knew she could stretch that for four meals or more and finally, she was at her limit and hoped she didn't go over. The kids were standing there looking sullen.

"I want some snacks and deserts, Mommy. Is this all we are getting? There are no fun foods in there only yucky old stuff for us to eat." Morgan said as she pulled her bottom lip out and pulled her lips down.

"Excuse me, May I talk to you?"

Sally turned to face the woman who was asking her a question. "Oh, hi. Yeah sure."

" My name is Rebecca. I've been listening to you guys shop. It sounds like you are in a tough place financially and are having trouble buying food. I hear your little ones asking for special foods and you cannot buy them"

Sally merely nodded her head.

"I would like to help you. Let's go up and down the aisles and pick out some foods you all will enjoy and what's healthy for you. Please let me do this for you."

Sally was stunned, and she was almost speechless. "Um, well......you don't need to do that."

Rebecca smiled. "But I want to. I've been blessed to have enough money to do it. Please let me."

Sally didn't know what to say. "Um, O.K I guess."

"Come, let's start at the beginning."

They walked to the first aisle which was fresh fruit and vegetables.

"Kids, what fruits would you like?'"

"I want apples!" Megan yelled.

"I want banana's." Morgan yelled.

"Can I get grapes?" Toby asked.

"I want oranges," Lucas said

Rebecca smiled. "So, get those things and put them in the cart." The kids all grabbed what they wanted and put them in the cart.

Next, they walked to the cereal aisle. "Why don't each of you pick out a box of cereal you want?" Rebecca said.

Each child grabbed a box of cereal and put it in the cart.

Then they walked to the dinner aisle. "Pick out some things from this aisle. Please don't hold back. I am going to get you meat, too."

Sally picked out some elbow pasta, spaghetti, spaghetti sauce jars, sloppy joe cans, scalloped potatoes, carrots, corn, green beans, peas, sweet potatoes, apple sauce, and mixed fruit.

They walked to the meat section and Sally picked out four one-pound packages of ground beef, two packages of chicken breasts, a ham, two packages of pork chops, and two packages of hot dogs. Then they hit the bread aisle, and she got three loaves of bread, two packages of hot dog rolls, one package of hamburger rolls, two packages of bagels, and a loaf of Italian bread. Next, was the dairy section, and she picked out parmesan cheese powder, cheddar cheese, cheese slices, another dozen eggs, twelve containers of yogurt, cottage cheese, and another gallon of milk. She also got a big jar of peanut butter and a big jar of jelly. Next was the kid's favorite section, desserts. Rebecca told them to each pick out a dessert and two snacks each. The kids were wild with excitement and they each picked out what they wanted. The cart was getting pretty full. They got to the ice cream section and Rebecca told them to pick out two half gallon containers of ice cream. They agreed on chocolate and cookies and cream. Across from that was juice and soda and she told them to pick out two bottles of soda and three bottles of juice. They chose orange and root beer soda and apple, fruit punch and grape juice. By now, the cart was almost full and Sally couldn't believe this strange woman was doing this for them. They got to the register and put the food on the moving belt. It came to $155 and Sally's eyes were wide as Rebecca pulled out a debit card and paid for the food. She was glad they were in Aldis where the food was so cheap.

"Thank you. I don't know what to say. This is amazing and so very kind of you. You don't even know us."

Rebecca smiled. "I am going to give you my phone number and I would like to get yours if that's O.K."

"Um, yeah that's O.K. Here's my phone number." And she wrote on a piece of paper and handed it to Rebecca and took Rebecca's number and put it on her phone.

They talked briefly and Sally told her what was going on in her life and Rebecca told her a little about herself. They parted, and each walked to their cars. Sally put the kids in the car and then loaded up the groceries. She almost ran out of room in the van for the food. They drove home, and she took the kids into the house, and then she brought all the food inside. It took her a while to put everything away and by the time she was done, she had tears in her eyes. The kids all came into the kitchen.

"I want to eat. I'm hungry! I want some of the yummy food we bought." Morgan said.

"Me too!" Toby and Lucas yelled together.

"Mommy, why did that woman buy us all this food?" Megan asked, and put her hands on her hips.

Sally clasped her hands behind her back. "I don't know Megan. She was being nice and felt bad we had little money for food. She said she had enough money, so she wanted to share it with us. There are some good people in the world."

Sally made the children peanut butter and jelly sandwiches and apple juice. After they finished, they each chose a dessert to finish their meal. She had to be at work in an hour. Her mom was coming to watch the kids. Her mom also was poor and couldn't help them with money. Her dad had died when she was young and her mom had raised her and her brother as a single mother. Her brother was selfish and even though he had money, he rarely helped her out. She worked as a cashier at Wal-Mart and usually got thirty-two hours a week and she made $12.50 an hour. She got some money from her husband but it wasn't much. She didn't have money for a lawyer to take him to court to get more. He gave her $75 a week, and it was used towards utilities for her apartment. After work, she headed home and her mom had the kids in bed. She took a shower and got dressed for bed and then after cleaning up the kid's toys, she retired to bed herself.

****

A week later, she got a phone call, and it was Rebecca.

"Hi. Sally, how are you? How is the food holding up?"

"I'm doing good. We still have a lot left. I am trying to ration it and make it last as long as possible."

"That's awesome. Let me know when you start running out. I wanted to talk to you about something. I thought of a way I can help you long term and not just with food and this should solve all your money problems. My dad needs a receptionist for his company and the pay is $24 an hour, and it's 40 hours a week and you would work 9 am until 5 pm. What do you think about that?"

Sally was speechless for a moment. "That's double what I make an hour now plus it's eight more hours a week. That's an amazing salary for a receptionist, but I've never done that before."

"My dad pays his employees well and takes good care of them. And the current receptionist said she would train you for seven days before she leaves."

Sally put her hand to her heart. "I'm speechless. This is an answer to my prayers and I promise I will put my all into it and be the best employee possible. I won't let such a great opportunity pass by me and I love the hours and so will my mother who watches my children for me."

"That's amazing to hear. You can start tomorrow. I want to take you food shopping one time to hold you until your first paycheck comes. I can meet you at Aldis tomorrow after you get off of work. I can meet you there at 5:30 pm."

Sally ran her fingers through her hair. "I can do that. Thank you so much for all you've done. I can never repay you."

"I expect nothing except for you, just to do your best at the job and as a mom. You are brave and amazing to do this all on your own. I don't think I could do it."

Sally smiled. "Thank you so much. I will see you tomorrow then." She hung up the phone.

Sally sat there and started crying. Her money troubles were going to be over and she could feed her children well. She went to bed early that night to be fresh and ready for her new job.

****

Sally had been working at her new job for six months and was doing great. She had gotten a raise and now makes $24 an hour. She didn't need to tell her children no all the time and could indulge them a little here and there. Her husband had served her with divorce papers and Rebecca had enlisted her family's lawyer to help Sally pro bono with her divorce proceedings. With a lawyer by her side, she was able to get a decent amount of child support and also alimony. She would be getting $350 a week from her husband instead of the measly $75 he was giving her. She had more than enough money for herself and her five kids. She owed it all to a kind woman who reached out to her when she was at her lowest and gave her a leg up.

Rebecca smiled at the memory and knew she had helped this woman and her children have a better life.

But, then she saw what would have happened if she had not intervened in this family's lives.

CHAPTER TWELVE

Sally got up before her five kids and walked into the kitchen. The kids would be up soon and would be demanding breakfast. She looked in her cabinets and all she could find was a half-empty box of generic Cheerios and half of a quart of milk. That would need to be shared four ways, and she was so glad that she was still nursing the baby even though she was two years old. She could get away with giving her a handful of cereal. She got the bowls out and rationed out the cereal n four bowls and left a small amount she put on the highchair. She waited to put the milk on so it wouldn't get soggy. But she didn't need long to wait because she heard the patter of little steps. Her sons Toby and Lucas came into the kitchen. Right after them, the twins, Morgan and Megan, came bounding into the room. They all took their seats and the complaints started.

"I don't want icky Cheerios for breakfast. I want a sweet cereal that's fun." Megan whined and complained.

"There's hardly any cereal in the bowl, Mom. I'm hungry and I want more." Morgan demanded and pounded the table with her fist

"I want marshmallows in my cereal and there's none here. I want something different." Lucas said with a pout on his face.

THE THINGS I NEVER KNEW |143

Toby put his napkin over the bowl and hung his head down.

Sally sighed. "I'm sorry guys, this is all I have to give you. I wish it could different but I have little money." She thought of all the money her husband had and the $75 he had been giving her a week and silently raged inside.

She poured the milk into the bowls in even amounts and it barely made the cereal wet. She might as well have not given them any. Tears formed in her eyes, but the kids didn't see it. She saw an eight ounce bottle of expressed breast milk and added it to their cereal. She would nurse the baby after she ate her dry cereal.

Morgan looked at her bowl and narrowed her eyes at her mother. "Hey, there's almost no milk in my bowl. I need more than this."

"There is no more, Morgan. I'm sorry and if I had more, I would give you more. Please don't make me feel any worse than I already do."

Megan stirred her cereal with a frown on her face. "There is just a tiny bit in here, you need to give me more."

The boys started eating their cereal and didn't complain but the expressions on their faces told a different story. Toby's lips drooped and Lucas's lips quivered. She felt like a horrible mother.

The kids moaned and groaned but ate the cereal they were given. Sally rummaged through her pocketbook to see how much money she had to go to the store. She counted all her paper bills and change and it came to $25.60. She decided she would go to Aldis supermarket where she could get the most for her money. She dreaded bringing the kids because she knew they would ask and beg for things she couldn't get for them. She loaded them in the car when they finished eating and drove off to the store. When they arrived, she got them out of the car and they strolled into the store. She went right to the dinner section, and she picked out three 12 packs of Ramen Noodles for $1.79 each. She got six boxes of macaroni and cheese that were 50 cents each. Then they walked to the cereal section, and she got a big box of Corn Flakes for $1.79. Next was the dairy section, and she grabbed a gallon of whole milk for $3.69 and a two dozen eggs for 79 cents each dozen. She walked to the canned vegetables and picked out carrots, corn, peas, and mixed vegetables for 59 cents each. Next, she got two one-pound bags of white rice for 79 cents each bag. She knew she was at her limit.

"I want some snacks and dessert. You only got yucky food." Megan complained.

Morgan held her fist up in the air. "I want dessert too! You got nothing good, only food we always eat."

Sally calculated her purchases in her head and knew she was close, too close but she walked them over to the snack section.

"You can pick out ONE dessert for all of you. It has to be under one dollar."

The kids raced up and down, demanding what they wanted. Each one wanted something different.

"O.K I am going to decide. We will get a big package of cookies because they have quite a bit in them and they are 99 cents. We will get vanilla creme cookies. That's enough for several meals. I will also get this big bag of popcorn kernels for 69 cents and we can make popcorn quite a few times." She prayed she had enough for them.

They walked to the checkout line, and she put her food on the conveyer belt. She held her breath as the foods were scanned and the total kept rising higher and higher. Finally, the total came out. $25.24 and she let her breath out. They barely made it since she had $25.60. She paid, and they walked to the van. She loaded the kids in and after the food and drove home. She got more than she thought she would but it would need to last until next week. She brought the kids into the house and then the food. As she put the food away, she calculated how it would last for various meals. She had half a loaf of bread and half a jar of peanut butter and half a jar of jelly. That would have to do for lunches. She made them each a half of a sandwich and called them to the table.

"I only get a half of a sandwich? I want a whole one, I am starving." Morgan whined.

"Me too! I am too big for only a half of a sandwich!" Megan said.

"I am sorry guys, that's all I have for you. Tomorrow is school and you will get a good breakfast and lunch. Here, you can receive three cookies each for dessert. That will fill you up and I will make a big bowl of popcorn for a snack today." Sally said.

Sally finished feeding the kids and was thankful she had food at all. She got paid the next week and her husband was going to give her $75 but almost all of it was going towards rent and utilities. She prayed the gas in her car was going to last until then. She had no money for a lawyer to try to get more money from her husband and she hoped the family court would listen to her without a lawyer. Her husband had his own lawyer, and she knew she was going to get burned. She just wanted to make it until payday.

****

It was almost a week later and most of the food she bought was gone. Tonight she was giving the kids corn flakes for dinner and there was just enough milk to cover the cereal. She still had plenty of popcorn left to make a big bowl and she hoped that would fill the kids up. Tomorrow was payday but the rent was due and it was $500. She had a tiny 1 bedroom apartment, and the kids got the bedroom and she slept on the couch. She had started another part-time job working at the Dollar Tree and was so grateful her mother babysat. Her job at Wal-Mart gave her 32 hours a week and the job at Dollar Tree gave her 16 hours. She worked 8 am till 4 pm four days a week at Wal Mart and she worked two days a week 8 am to 4 pm at the Dollar Tree. She got 1 day off a week and she still barely made ends meet. She had a talk with her husband and told him that she should not be totally supporting the children while he gave her $300 a month for five of them. He smugly told her she should be grateful for what she got. He took the kids every other weekend from Friday until Sunday and half the time was late picking them up, sometimes missing a day and not getting them until Saturday afternoon. It was hard on her and suddenly the floor was jerked from under her. Today at work, her cash register drawer was $40 short, and she did not have the money on her to cover it. She knew she did not steal and must have made a mistake somehow. But because of that, she was fired from Wal-Mart. She didn't know what she was going to do. She scrambled and put in applications to a variety of places but knew if they questioned Wal Mat about why she was fired, it would not appear good for her. She prayed as she had never prayed before.

****

One month later her bank account was at zero and her cabinets and fridge were empty, she only had $200 a week and the rent was overdue. Her landlord said he would start eviction papers if he did not get his money in

3 days. She still could not find another job. She told her husband he was going to need to take the kids if she had to move in with her mother. Her mom had a tiny one-bedroom apartment. He laughed at her and told her that was not going to happen. She sat on the couch, crying.

"Mommy, why are you crying?" Megan asked.

"Mommy is having trouble paying our bills sweetie, and she is scared."

"I thought daddy paid the bills."

Sally gave a mirthless laugh. "No, sweetie. Mommy pays for almost everything."

"Why can't daddy live with us and help us then?" Morgan asked, and cocked her head to one side.

"He doesn't want to. It's not mommy's choice." Sally could have added that he had a new girlfriend who moved in with him but she did not."

Sally had talked to her mom, and she said they could all squeeze into her apartment as a last resort but maybe they could search for a bigger place for all of them to live together. Then there was a knock on the door. She walked to the door and answered it and there was a lady standing there with a clipboard.

"Hello, are you Sally Fontana?"

"Um, yeah I am."

"My name is Jessica Lewis and I am from Child Protective Services. Your kid's school reported that the children were complaining they do not get enough food to eat. May I come in to talk?"

Sally's face went pale. "Um, sure."

"First, before we sit down, I want to see your cabinets and refrigerator for food," Jessica said.

Sally led her to the kitchen and showed her the empty cabinets and almost empty fridge.

They walked into the living room and sat down.

"Why do you not have food for your kids? What were you planning on feeding them tonight?"

Sally stared at her hands. "I lost my job. I was going to give them some Ramen Noodles for dinner."

"But there were only two packages of the noodles. You have five children. Why don't you get food stamps?"

Sally wrung her hands. "My husband hasn't divorced me and we haven't filed for legal separation so it goes by his salary, which is way too much for food stamps. It's the same with the food bank."

Jessica frowned. "Why does your husband not give you enough money to feed the kids?"

Sally got a hard expression on her face. "He gives us $75 a week for all five kids. That goes towards paying the bills. And we are going to be evicted from our apartment if I don't pay the rent in three days. Well, he will start the paperwork anyway."

"Why haven't you filed for separation?"

"My husband hates me and is saying he won't sign anything. He is trying to make our lives impossible." Sally looked up at the ceiling and closed her eyes.

Jessica narrowed her eyes. "So, where do you plan on living?"

"I might need to move in with my mother and then maybe search for a bigger place for the seven of us."

Jessica shook her head. "Well, the place needs to be big enough and I will need to see what it is and inspect it. You have a case with us now and it will be founded since you truly don't have enough food to feed your children in the home. I will give you a $25 food voucher and you can go tomorrow to the food bank and get some food. I will be in touch with you tomorrow to discuss what needs to be done."

Sally breathed a sigh of relief that the kids weren't being taken away. "Thank you. I am doing my best. I actually haven't eaten in almost three days so my kids will have the food."

Jessica nodded. "That's commendable but I hope you won't need to do that." Then she left.

Sally was feeling dizzy from not eating. She got up to go to the kitchen to make dinner for the children. As she was standing by the stove, everything started to spin and dark spots appeared before her eyes and she collapsed to the floor, striking her head on the corner of the fridge. After that, she saw nothing.

"Mommy, mommy are you O.K? Wake up! Wake up NOW!" Morgan said in a frantic voice.

The kids gathered around her but she did not wake up. The kids sat there for hours only getting up to go to the bathroom. Finally, at midnight, they all laid down on the couch and fell asleep. The next morning, she still was not awake and Morgan decided to go to the neighbor to get help. The ambulance came and Sally was taken to the hospital in a coma. After three days she woke but she had some brain damage and needed rehabilitation. Her mother had the children and decided to move into Sally's apartment and let hers go. She brought with her the sleeper couch she had and she and Sally, when Sally came home, slept on that. Sally was never the same and had to go on disability, her husband finally divorced her, and she was able to get the help she needed from the government. Her children grew up in poverty. Megan became a drug addict and Morgan got pregnant at age fourteen. The boys managed to grow up unscathed and the baby, with Down Syndrome, moved to live in a group home. Sally's mom lived to help raise the kids but died soon after from heart disease. The family's sad ending was made worse because they could not get a hand up and help when they first needed it.

Rebecca's eyes were opened to what could have happened if she had not intervened in their lives. She shook her head in wonder.

CHAPTER THIRTEEN

Rebecca thought she was useless in life and didn't deserve heaven. She never realized all the people she helped and the lives she changed for the better. She was a good person who lived out the Golden Rule and followed the commandments of Jesus. There would have been so much more loss and so much more pain in people's lives if she had not been born and had not reached deep within herself to help others. Her eyes were opened and she had peace knowing she did deserve her crown, her robe, and her place in heaven. Jesus made it clear she deserved the words "Well done, my good and faithful servant."

The End

Thank you for reading my book and I hope you enjoyed it! If you did, can you please leave me a review on Amazon? It only takes a minute. This really helps me out with book sales and would be highly appreciated! Your review will mean the world to me!

Contact Jennifer Ann Corgan

Email
contact@jennifercorgan.com

Website
http://Jennifercorgan.net

Follow me on:

Instagram
@jenniferanncorganauthor

Facebook
@jennifercorganauthor

Jennifer is also a copywriter, freelance writer, and digital marketer. She creates blog posts, articles, SEO website content optimization, whitepapers, case studies, e-books, lead magnets, sales letters, website content, ghostwriting, social media management, email management, and paid ads management

She has branched out to do Amazon Keyword and Category Research for Authors.

COMING SOON
Shattered Family

Freedom is a distant memory of the past that only fools wish for. Those who want to stay alive, know better than to wish for their freedom.

When the country was seized and overthrown by a coup, few expected such drastic measures. The land of the free, the home they once knew, is long gone. No longer are they free to speak openly or be who they want. Their lives are in the hands of the newly formed government.

Drug use results in the death penalty, children are taken away for having religious knowledge, and all churches must be approved by the government. Not even your own home is safe. Black boxes listen to everything you say within your own walls and birth control chips in your arm ensure you have no way of having a baby without government consent.

Mind Reform Institutes are springing up across the country, designed to brainwash the citizens into following the government's rules. When Grace dares to teach her young daughter about religion, her daughter is taken away and Grace is sent to one of the institutes.

Doug was not a man to be cowed by the new laws, still speaking openly against the government. It was only a matter of time before he is taken to an institute, his girlfriend shipped off with him for committing crimes of her own.

Though the crimes that have been committed seem small, their side effects are starting to trickle through the family, robbing others of what they want most.

With their placements in the Mind Reform Institutes, the game of survival has started, each person questioning what sacrifices they are willing to make to stay alive.

May/June 2022

More Books by
Jennifer Ann Corgan

Runaway Secrets

Breaking the Ties That Bind

No Other Choice

Against the Odds

I Am A Copywriter: What's Your Superpower?

I am A Natural Health Expert: What's Your Super Power?

Sexual Assault, Sexual Abuse and Mental Health Comprehensive Resource Guide

GET THEM ON AMAZON!

www.ingramcontent.com/pod-product-compliance
Lightning Source LLC
Chambersburg PA
CBHW022019170626
46808CB00003B/982